Stepping Out

W · W · NORTON & COMPANY · INC · NEW YORK

STEPPING OUT

A LOVE STORY

ROLAINE HOCHSTEIN

To Sara Weinberger Abrahams and Martin R. Abrahams,
my parents, who gave me an education,
and to Mort Hochstein, my husband,
who encouraged me to use it.

STEPPING OUT

CHAPTER 1

When she finally fell in love—helplessly, hopelessly, shatteringly—with a man old enough almost to be her father, Beverly Peck Gordon learned to be proud of her son's Bar Mitzvah but for reasons entirely different from those behind her original pride and subsequent chagrin. The man she fell for, an even less likely lover than she was, he being a Mayflower descendant and a pillar of a decidedly Presbyterian community, an intellectual and a stoic, turned her right side up by his clear-sighted, unforced, and matter-of-fact recognition of most of the things she had been spending her life trying to prove to people like him. This overturning, this Wasp's-eye

view, came magically upon her, certainly not from reasoned
debate or even sweet persuasion. For when they spoke, between transports of reverential and ecstatic lovemaking and
interludes of rapt, wondrous silence, what Beverly and her
white-haired lover with the Plymouth Rock profile said was
likely to be inconsequential, as was fitting for people who did
not belong in one another's future.

Long before she fell in love and blew the house down,
Beverly Peck Gordon had been an officer in the Temple
Sholom Sisterhood, a model modern Jewish housewife who,
as legions of Marjorie Morningstars had done before her, had
hemmed off her adventures, frozen her fantasies along with
trays of the next weekend's desserts, and blown herself up with
the acceptable satisfaction of wholeheartedly caring for her
home, husband, and children. For such a woman as Beverly
had become, the Bar Mitzvah of her firstborn son, Sanford
Mark Gordon, was the glorious culmination of thirteen years
of solicitude and one of the greatest pleasures life offered,
second only to the wedding of a daughter, which could be
anticipated in another ten years when Beverly's second and
lastborn, Allison Deborah Gordon, would be twenty-one.

"We had light blue tablecloths and dark blue napkins with
matching menus and matchboxes," Beverly told Harvey Porter as she lay in his arms in the polished brass bed in his room
at the Madison Hotel. "One hundred fifty guests. Continental
service. The waiters wore white gloves."

Harvey Porter, who had read about the Bar Mitzvah cus-
tom in an illustrated anthropology book with slick, oversized
pages, listened dreamily. He pictured the noble gathering but
saw, superimposed like a musical leitmotif, his own dear Bev-

erly moving among the tables radiantly, competently, making everyone comfortable. "Both my daughters were married in church," he said. "We had small receptions at home. I wish we could have had a big splashy party like yours. It sounds so warm and wonderful."

Beverly didn't even look to see if he was putting her on. She already knew after three days in Washington, sitting on the steps of the Jefferson Memorial (that he loved and she hated), standing outside the Hirshhorn Gallery examining the Ipousteguy man-in-a-door sculpture (that she loved and he hated), eating crabcakes (mostly she), drinking Old-Fashioneds (mostly he), walking, talking, admiring the skeletons f cherry trees against a bleak autumn sky (which they both loved), that he didn't see anything either ridiculous or reprehensible about her ethnic past. She had no need to defend herself from Harvey Porter. She had no wish to crack wise. He had completely disarmed her.

She had given him three chances. Prowling suspiciously among the national monuments and rhapsodically among the art treasures, Beverly had put her patriotic companion, a bust of whom could easily have passed as one of the early Presidents, through three crucial tests. Along the steps, lobbies, rotundas, corridors, chambers, galleries, terraces, paths, lawns, and sidewalks of their country's capital, Harvey Porter had three chances to prove his innate sense of superiority to her and her Jewish kind.

She had let him know early on, as she always let all Gentiles know early on, before they had the opportunity to embarrass themselves and outrage Beverly with some of their choice remarks about *some Jew who* or *you know those New Yorkers* or, still more subtly, with smiles of mutual sympathy, *those people*, so that Beverly would have to shoot back and say "*Who do you mean—the blacks or the Jews?*" unless her antagonist was either black or Jewish and she could then assume he meant members of the other group, though the assumption was not always correct. So, to avoid discomfort, she had told this fair-skinned, blue-eyed, gentle-mannered lawyer from Connecticut, who had offered to share his taxi in the rain, that she was wild for the work of Edgar Degas even though he was a known anti-Semite.

"I didn't know that about Degas," Harvey Porter, whose own name she didn't yet know, had said, not put off by her statement, not even taking it as a personal revelation. "I know he was obsessed by ballet dancers."

Point One for Porter, though he didn't actually introduce himself until they were having lunch among sequined cushions in a scented alcove of a highly decorated Hindustani health restaurant on P Street, near Dupont Circle. "By the way," he said, wryly surprised at himself for having forgotten something so pertinent. The name brought to Beverly's mind pictures of Early American people and places, with their sharp outlines and clear colors, their straightforward design. She told Harvey Porter about her son's strong interest in American history, a high school subject that had eluded hers. "I've always preferred European," she said, confessing a taste for the oblique and opaque. "Probably because I'm Jewish." She flung it like a gauntlet but he picked it up and handed it back, a clean, lacy handkerchief.

"You're Jewish!" he said. His eyes were bright with interest. "I live such a provincial life, in such a small village, that I almost never come across any Jewish people."

She sat back and waited.

"When I went to law school in New Haven, there were a number of Jewish students in my classes. It was a pleasure to be with them. They were very bright."

Beverly looked him straight in the eye. "Didn't it bug you just a little bit?"

He seemed not to understand.

"You know. All those smartass, bigmouth Jewish kids? Smarter than the teacher? Taking over the class?"

"Oh, no. I loved it," Harvey Porter said in his straightforward way. "The Jewish boys made the class interesting and I believe the teachers liked it, too. They were curious, you see. They wanted to get *at* things. It was stimulating for all of us."

She was ashamed of having tried to bait him.

That was Point Two. She didn't have the heart to keep up the attack. She discarded the obvious follow-up questions about Porter versus Jew lawyer in adversary situations. Apparently, he came from a small, remote square on the New England map and did not often find himself in hotheaded courtroom battle. Thomas Jefferson had been a lawyer, too, and a hypocrite, as Beverley had read somewhere, for keeping slaves while he popped off against slavery.

So she gave this New England gentleman, this kindly fellow, this terribly nice chap just one more chance to show himself as just one more Wasp son-of-a-bitch like the ladies at the information desk at the Metropolitan Museum of Art in New York City, the society ladies with straight hair and skinny legs, who wore skirts and sweaters or baggy knit dresses and were always right in their dry Katharine Hepburn voices while Beverly, even in her most restrained, fastidious, and unobtrusive Reform Jew costume, was always irremediably and unredeemedly wrong.

At night, under the high-class colonial chandelier of the Montpelier Restaurant, while Harvey Porter was downing an after-dinner cognac and Beverly was clinging to her profiterole plate, taking tiny mouthfuls of equal parts chocolate sauce, cream puff shell, and vanilla ice cream, she noticed that her companion fitted right in with the restrained luxury of the paneled walls and the tall, scalloped draperies, the fine iron grillwork of the stair rail, and the handsome candled sconces, and that his shirt under his dark, tasteful tie was as white as the linen tablecloth under the silver coffee service, and she decided to tell him about her last visit to the Metropolitan Museum. She watched the waiter pour cream into her third cup of coffee and then she told Harvey Porter how, only last week, waiting for her friend Mollie Parish to meet her for lunch, she was standing beside the round front information desk with its inner circle of clearly social women doing their bit of noblesse oblige by handing out floor plans and Calendars of Events to all oncoming culture seekers regardless of rank and she had distinctly heard a Radcliffe braid-around-the-head complain to a Bryn Mawr ponytail about those terrible mornings "when the entire B'nai B'rith of Mount Kisco comes down on you." Beverly had stood by, hearing this with mute, frustrated rage.

"Isn't the B'nai B'rith a men's club?" Harvey Porter asked as he had asked her earlier in the long evening what was the difference between bigarade and Montmorency *vis-à-vis* roast duck.

"Yes, but it's a *Jewish* men's club," Beverly said as clearly as she had said before: "Oranges and cherries."

"She might as well have said Elks, then." (He had ordered roast prime ribs, after all. She had the duck bigarade and had put a generous sample on his plate.) "I should think it would have bothered you more if she'd been putting down a women's group."

He lost the challenge. He lost his chance. He lost brilliantly, this hick, this dope, this backwoodsman who didn't know the difference between sexism and anti-Semitism. He lost his place in any nook, cranny, slot, or pigeonhole she had reserved for him. He lost his Protestant face, his pillory, his pedestal, her prejudice. But he won Beverly for once and for always. Stripped of her fighting gear, her great wailing wall of defense with its burs and needles, Beverly was soft and yielding as a baby bird and sweet as field flowers. Harvey Porter had lost all his points but Beverly looked behind his intelligent, somewhat perplexed blue eyes and saw such purity and simplicity that in the taxi on the way to her hotel, she took a second look at the Jefferson Memorial and thought she might try, in the future, to be a little more charitable in her consideration of the Master of Monticello.

"Families like mine never get together," Harvey Porter said two beautiful days later, after he'd put on the robe he'd bought at Garwood's that afternoon with Beverly choosing the red velours over a green chambray. She, lying still robeless and Rubensy in his arms, told him about her son's Bar Mitzvah. Her description omitted the wisecracks and rollicking irony that had delighted so many of her various audiences in the three years since the Bar Mitzvah had turned her upside down.

Everyone agreed that it was a great Bar Mitzvah. Plenty of food. Everything delicious. It was a beautiful place, this country club, and everybody was there from both sides. Peter Gordon was evidently doing very well. The Bar Mitzvah boy, Sanford, was a real little gentleman. He had carried himself beautifully in the Temple, read the Hebrew without a mistake that anyone could pick up, and was a pleasure at the reception, where he shook hands with all the aunts and uncles and second cousins who remembered him from when he was a little pisher, laughed at the weak jokes of the crinkled, strong-smelling, jowly old men, and thanked everybody earnestly for the envelopes they pushed into his suit jacket pocket that was already beginning to look like a mail pouch.

The day of Sanford Mark Gordon's Bar Mitzvah was the happiest day of his mother's life, with the possible exceptions of her wedding day fifteen years earlier and the days on which her children were born. One week after the Bar Mitzvah—this great event, this *simche*, this puberty rite, potlatch, gathering of clans, show-and-tell to beat all, this culmination of an attentively parented childhood and well-provided-for wifehood, this solemn temple ceremony followed by the most festive of catered luncheons for one hundred and fifty nearest and dearest friends and relatives of the Pecks and the Gordons—a short seven days later, Beverly, the Bar Mitzvah mother, looked back on the occasion as the nadir of a life of cowardice and self-deception.

During the months that followed, as she struggled to haul herself up from the depths of her Bar Mitzvah depression, Beverly saw the causes of her fall in many different lights.

What could be wrong with a Bar Mitzvah?
Sexism.

Beverly, gracious hostess, wore a smartly understated, one-hundred-and-eighty-five-dollar Teal Traina dress, fifty-dollar pumps dyed to match, a forty-dollar (wholesale) handbag, a twenty-dollar casual hairdo, not to mention hat and gloves and her two-carat engagement ring and real cultured pearls, none of which she had paid for with a penny of her own money. "I never felt more like a kept woman," she confessed to her sisters in oppression at the Consciousness-Raising group she attended once a week for several supportive months. Her sisters understood perfectly, which is more than her husband did. ("You'll still have me to take care of," he told her, thinking she was distraught at the prospect of her children growing up.)

What could be wrong with a Bar Mitzvah?
Identity crisis.

She mentioned it to the stoop-shouldered psychiatrist who scared her away in a single visit by offering her pills when what she really wanted was to tell him how awful she felt and find out why. The Bar Mitzvah had reminded her that she was in danger of growing old before she grew up. "Thirty-eight years old and still a G movie," Beverly wept into the Kleenex extended by Dr. Stucke. She sat disconsolately still in the Early American rocker in his Early American office with an irritating wrought-iron eagle looking down on her, and tried to tell how she had sat, in the front pew, as her son in his new blue suit and his father's tie had come to stand before the Torah and how she who never prayed to the Temple's God found herself praying to the springs of the cosmos that her boy would not forget the words he had been phonetically memorizing for the past six months and how she felt his life

inside her and felt the memory of his first prenatal nudgings as
he helped to unroll the Torah scroll and took hold of the silver
pointer by which the Law was traditionally read. She could not
quite describe to the kindly, non-directive shrink how, when
before beginning his reading, her son had looked straight at
her with a serenely confident, generously loving smile in his
eyes, she had felt so expanded by a warmth of pride and joy
that she thought she would float to the domed ceiling and
from there light up the whole of Temple Sholom. She tried to
explain how this elation, this good-mother, good-daughter,
good-Jewish-girl character had swollen to a burst of pride with
pieces of her personality spattered all over the house. She
couldn't tell him how terrible she felt but "You're a psychiatrist," she told him, "so you probably know better than I do."

What could be wrong with a Bar Mitzvah?
Conspicuous consumption.

They didn't believe her anyway, her classmates from
graduate school. Sitting on the floor of an inner-city apartment, with Terri and Joe and Tom and Paula from her poetry
seminar, all of them in variations on the theme of bluejeans
and work shirts, sitting cross-legged and drinking Almadén red
from paper cups, she swore she had once—not very long
ago—been a hostess at a party that began with a wine-and-hors
d'oeuvres reception downstairs at the temple, a tremendous
crowd around a little table while the cantor blessed the bread
and the wine and everybody grabbed a little something to eat
so they wouldn't be famished on the two-mile trip to the country club where a real luncheon awaited them, preceded by
cocktails and more hors d'oeuvres, this time fancy hot and

cold, passed around by smiling waitresses in ruffled white aprons. Tom Dalton, who used to play in a rock band and do peyote, couldn't picture his sympathetic friend and ardent fellow student presiding over a lunch at which white-gloved waiters shoved stuffed derma on the sides of gold-rimmed plates already heaped with filet mignon, potato puffs, puree of broccoli, and braised celery hearts (not to mention the side dishes) while people like Beverly's Uncle Harold stood up and yelled "What the hell kind of party is this they give only one piece stuffed derma?" It was all too true, Beverly told them, but the kids from the Contemporary Poetry seminar attributed the description to the fruitful imagination she had already displayed in her classroom interpretation of the works of Wallace Stevens, another member of the inscrutable bourgeoisie.

The truth was that she had loved it all, the whole production. From making up the guest list to sending out the last thank-you note. She had loved saying Yes. Yes to every relative her mother wanted to invite and then Yes to the Gordon family because you can't do for one side and not the other. Yes, she had said to the blue-on-blue invitation cards, Yes to the baked alaska for dessert, Yes to the daisy and carnation centerpieces for every table, Yes to the dance band Sandy wanted, Yes to Allison's request for a table of her own friends, and, finally, Yes to Peter—her dear, generous, loving husband when he asked if she had taken care of everything.

She had loved every minute, from the early-morning arrival of the first guests to the late-evening departure of the last. She had loved even the temple Sabbath services, which seemed, on this day, unusually pungent with relevant and universal truths, the rabbi especially articulate, the cantor in extraordinarily good voice. She loved seeing her son, who didn't know a word of Hebrew and had failed to absorb either the facts or the essence of Jewish history, stand bravely beaming his happiness as he was joined on the pulpit for a blessing by his Grandpa Ben, who didn't know much Hebrew either, and his Grandpa Max, who did. She had loved watching her daughter Allison, in her first pair of pantyhose and a dress that stretched tightly across her round belly, sit gravely and attentively through the worship, and then, when the occasion called, turn magically into a little hostess, a junior Beverly, remembering names, performing introductions, giving and receiving kisses and compliments, and bringing to her parents enough mined bliss to last until the next major celebration.

She had loved the look on Peter's face, of dazed pleasure and overwhelmed satisfaction. Peter, who always looked as young and strong and desirable to her as he had on the day, fifteen years before, when they had stood together in front of a different rabbi and promised to cherish one another until death, seemed too bright and fresh to be the father of a Bar Mitzvah boy and the sponsor (to the extent of three thousand dollars' worth of single-handed hard work) of this affair. When they danced together, after Beverly had danced with Sandy and Peter had danced with Allison and Sandy with Allison and Grandpa Ben with Grandma Sadie and Grandpa Ben with Grandma Sadie and Allison and Beverly, and Grandpa Max all by himself with his cane, Beverly was proud and happy to be in the arms of her good-looking, light-moving, sweet-smelling husband who seemed to have inside his skin—from his curly black hair to his size-eleven feet—countless cunning and sensuous hooks that kept her caught to him, as much a mystery to her as on the day they were married.

The lovely family sat tall in the front pew of Temple Sholom, so cool in its decor and its congregation so decorous. Rabbi Blackman, wholesome, clean-shaven, imposing in his black robes, a gentle man without the trace of a foreign accent, smiled a personal greeting down at them as the service began.

How goodly are thy tents, O Jacob, thy dwellings, O Israel! Through Thy great mercy, O God, I come to Thy house and bow down in Thy holy temple in the fear of Thee.

Peter Gordon sat tall and dark in the front row of this handsome modern temple, where his children went more or less regularly to Sunday school and where he himself showed up on High Holidays and occasionally on Friday nights in between to pray to he knew not what. He had so much to be thankful for; he had achieved so much for himself and his family. Beverly's joy increased at the sight of his broad smile, recently perfected by an excellent capping job. She knew that his happiness was in her and the children. Peter had often said it: Beverly was the rock of his life, a woman of valor, worth more than rubies and pearls. She took hold of his hand.

Help us, O God, to banish from our hearts all vainglory, pride of worldly possessions, and self-sufficient leaning upon our own reason. Fill us with the spirit of meekness and the grace of modesty that we may grow in wisdom and in reverence. May we never forget that all we have and prize is but lent to us.

The Rabbi, Beverly was thinking, is a man the children can look up to. She had gone temple-shopping, when they moved to Heightsville, for a place that would be a good influence on the children. She and Peter had attended services at four or five different Reform and Conservative temples in the county and were convinced after two visits and earnest

research that Rabbi Blackman and Temple Sholom were the
man and the place to which they could make an honest com-
mitment. That was the way Peter had put it. Membership was,
of course, primarily for the children's education, but of course
Beverly was soon drawn into Sisterhood activities and she and
Peter occasionally partook of the social and cultural events,
though lately Peter, pursued by rising expenses, hardly had
time to turn around, much less go to parties. A long way they
had both come—Beverly from the immigrants' Bronx, Peter
from a small town where his grandfather had parlayed
backpack peddling into a pushcart and then a little store and
now a big store that made a handy living for Peter's sister and
her husband, who sat at that moment a few rows back dressed
in their finest for the rich brother's party. Here was Peter
himself, the head of a fine, well-behaved family, worrying only
that his son should remember his passage and t at he himself
would not falter over the blessing or the honorary closing of
the Torah ark.

The congregation rose to the Rabbi's opening arms. The
Gordon family stood tall.

Shma Yisroel, adonoy elohanu, adonoy echod.

Hear, O Israel: The Lord our God, the Lord is One.

In a minute it would be time for Sandy to be called to the
Torah.

Thank God, Beverly said to herself upon arriving at the
Long Hill Country Club, where guests were already drinking
and picking at the trays of cold hors d'oeuvres. The restraint of
the decor pleased her, the quiet elegance of the long room into
which uniformed waitresses were beginning to slip from a
screened-off kitchen entrance to refill trays and pass around

the hot canapés. It was a very civilized affair.

Her father's cousin Della, a woman built and decorated like a pincushion, gave her a big hug. "It's a beautiful party, darling. You should be very proud."

A cousin of Peter's, older than Beverly, less formidable than Della, brown eyes soft under false lashes, took Beverly's two hands in hers. "Your son was beautiful. I'm so happy to be here to share this with you."

Stanley, a cousin's husband, kissed her on the mouth, kept his hand on her back, too low for comfort. "I got to thank you," he said, "for not seating us with my brother-in-law." *Brother-in-law* was uttered with zestfully primitive hatred.

Martha, Beverly's best friend since high school, stopped with a well-filled plate in one hand, a Scotch sour in the other. "You've done it," she said with sincere admiration. "Freddie says this is the first Bar Mitzvah he has ever really enjoyed."

Beverly was floating.

"And thanks for sitting us with the Parishes. They're lovely people."

While the luncheon was being served, Beverly moved from table to table, borne by the aura of her own sweetness. Even the kids, Sandy and his friends, Allison and hers, sat like satisfied poppets with their cheeks glowing from the excitement of the occasion and any hard liquor they may have coaxed out of complaisant bartenders.

Beverly's old Aunt Helen caught her hand. "Tell me, Beverly dear. Your Cousin Nadelman didn't come? He wasn't invited?"

"Of course he was invited," Beverly assured the anxious-faced old lady. "I even wrote a note that I'd have a kosher meal for him. But he said it was too far to come from Florida."

The aunt sighed one great sigh for all the dead and missing. "I hope he at least sent a generous gift," she said.

Gloria Levinson, the president of the Temple Sholom Sisterhood, said she had never tasted anything like the chicken strudel and asked for the name of the caterer.

Cousin Marilyn from Philadelphia said it was such a warm and friendly party she was glad she made the trip.

Cousin Mac from Huntington said that Beverly looked like a *Vogue* cover girl.

Aunt Pearl said that Allison was a little doll, the sweetest, prettiest, *nicest* little girl she had ever seen.

Uncle Sam said he ate everything and everything was good. Aunt Bertha said they would both have heartburn, but it would be worth it.

Peter's father wept with joy and said he only wished Peter's mother had lived to see this beautiful occasion. Peter's brother-in-law made a toast to the Bar Mitzvah boy and the Bar Mitzvah boy made a toast to his parents. They were a wonderful couple, he said, in the pompous, thrilled way of Bar Mitzvah boys, even if they were his own Mom and Dad. After he had cut the tiered and pillared, blue and white cake with thirteen candles lit by thirteen sets of relatives, and after dessert and coffee had been served and after guests had begun to leave, Sandy stood by Beverly and told her with shining eyes and a chesty voice that he really appreciated this party and would always remember it as the happiest day in his life.

And when they were all home again, sprawled out in the Gordons' family room with their shoes off and their feet up, Beverly's mother had nothing to complain about. "Everything was done with good taste," Grandma Sadie said. Beverly's triumph was complete. Sandy and his father counted up the gifts and it was announced that the Bar Mitzvah presents so far came to twenty-two hundred dollars in cash, stocks, and savings bonds, plus a number of personal gifts including electric shavers, gold cuff links, luggage, clock-radios, golf clubs, monogrammed shirts, gold-tooled leather studboxes, tennis rackets, scuba equipment, cashmere sweaters, and, of course, fountain pens.

"You know that presents are not the point," Peter told his children severely. He had drunk too much. His son had been given too much. Peter turned on the television to lose himself in the eleven-o'clock news.

"Don't worry about the money," Grandpa Max, Peter's father, said in the vague manner of the once powerful. "I'm going to give you a check will cover the whole thing." His daughter and son-in-law helped him out the door. "Sure, Pop," the son-in-law humored him. "You'll make it out in the morning." Allison and Sandy ran to the car to kiss him goodby. Beverly came out with a box of leftover cake.

After Grandma Sadie and Grandpa Ben had left, after Sandy and Allison finally calmed down and went to bed, Beverly sat on the edge of the couch where Peter had conked out watching the news.

"Put your arms around me," she said.

"Tell me you love me."

"Move over so I can give you a hug."

Peter remained conked out. Beverly made a tic-tac-toe of kisses along his cheek and Peter opened his eyes in bleary irritation. "I've been putting out all day long," he said. "Why don't you leave me alone?"

Beverly moved away.

"It was a good party," Peter said. "You did a good job."

Beverly began to empty ashtrays.

"I'm tired now," Peter said. "Can't you see I have nothing left?"

Beverly went into the kitchen.

"See you upstairs," Peter said.

That was the end of the day of the Bar Mitzvah, one of the four happiest days in the life of Beverly Peck Gordon.

Why, then, after she had stuffed the crown of her soft straw hat with tissue paper to hold its shape and tenderly replaced it in its box on the top shelf of her sliding-door closet

and put her hundred-and-eighty-five-dollar Teal Traina dress into a transparent garment bag and stored it behind other dressy dresses more often worn?

after, on the next day, she had telephoned the caterer to thank him for arranging a thoroughly satisfactory party

and shown Allison how to hand-wash pantyhose with cold water and Woolite liquid

and taken Sandy to the bank to open a special College Savings account with his cash and to put his stocks and bonds in the safe-deposit box

and stopped at the stationery counter of the Saks Fifth Avenue in the shopping mall to pick up her order of one hundred thank-you notes with Sandy's name in dark blue letters on the light blue paper?

and after, a day later, she had answered perhaps her thirtieth phone call of praise and congratulation

and had even been telephoned by a complete stranger who had heard about the wonderful affair and wanted to know where she could call to get the same three-piece combo for her son's Bar Mitzvah the following November?

after three, four, or five days of picking up the stitches of a fine, soft, and neatly patterned life that had slipped off the needle during the preparation and celebration,

why did she suddenly trip, slip, fall, hurtle, catapult into an abyss of such hopelessness, despair, and vile, sinking horror that all the leaves on the blooming trees around her custom-built house turned black overnight and the charming town of Heightsville became as remote and papery as an old movie set and all the eyes of all the people she met were desperate or desolate and she herself was filled with pity for her own children who were, like her and everybody else, doomed to a life of futility and inevitable death?

"I'm depressed," Beverly told her mother when Sadie called five days after the Bar Mitzvah to see why she hadn't heard from her daughter for so long.

Sadie had tried to be helpful. "You always get a little let down after a big occasion."

"It's worse than let down, Mom. I feel as if I'm in a terrible hole."

"So why don't you meet me in the city? We can go shopping."

"Thanks, Mom. It's very sweet of you, but I can hardly move. I think . . ." (she was so deeply depressed that she went ahead and said it) "I think I'm going to get my doctor to recommend a psychiatrist."

"A psychiatrist?" Now Sadie was horrified. "A psychiatrist for you? You must be crazy!"

CHAPTER 2

How does such a meeting happen?

A man and a woman stand, caught in the act of going different places, momentarily stopped, these two among the mill of people moving in all directions. Here they stand, stopped, on the strip of taxi platform that runs alongside the busy entrances and exits of National Airport. They stand on parallel points, equidistant from the curb, ten or twelve feet apart, with a clear field of space between them. A youngish, carelessly dressed woman; an oldish, carefully put together man. Action all around them and a quiet space between, broken only by the random cut of a fellow traveler coming or going across the strip. The man and the woman are both facing front, looking for a taxicab. Their turns are almost in unison. It is a cold fall day. Rain slants in under the strip of roof.

29

The clear field of space between them is needled with rain.

When the blue and yellow cab pulled up in front of Beverly, she stood away and pointed to the man down the line. "He was here first," she told the unbelieving driver.

Harvey Porter pulled back and performed a restrained stateside version of the *After you, Gaston* pantomime.

Beverly closed the space between them with the taxicab crawling along beside her.

"Listen," she told the oldish man. "I'm as strong as you are and there's no reason for you to give up a cab."

Harvey Porter smiled, showing sweetness and pipe-stained teeth. "I see," he said. "Thank you."

He settled himself on the back seat and then leaned out to ask, "Would it be acceptable, in that case, for me to give you a ride to where you're going?"

Cabs were being captured before they reached the strip. Beverly was very wet. Her hair was flopping over her forehead and dripping water in her eyes. She said, "Yes," and got in. She sat close to her corner, partly to keep from messing him up.

This distinguished-looking establishment type was orderly in a clean, pressed raincoat which seemed completely immune to moisture. She was soggy in a corduroy coat and walking shoes. She had collected all his rain. She took out some Kleenex and wiped her nose and her eyes. Then she said to her dry companion, "Look. If we get to where you're going first, I'd like to drop you off."

He seemed to think she was very delightful. "I'm going to Dupont Circle," he said.

"Great," she said.

She was going to the Phillips Art Gallery, a block from Dupont Circle and just around the corner from the office building where Harvey Porter was to meet one of his clients and another party who were about to enter into a contract. At Dupont Circle, the gentleman stepped out of the cab and reached for his wallet, but before he could pay, the woman had scrambled out beside him and was pushing a handful of bills at the driver, who had a Spanish accent and hair like a thatched roof and who was still trying to figure out the game of this wild little woman with the big mouth. There was a short, polite fight on the downtown corner of Massachusetts Avenue and the passengers ended up paying a full fare each, which irritated the gentleman but not the woman, who said with satisfaction, "Just consider it a big tip. I'm sure it won't spoil him."

She turned toward Twenty-first street. She was short and squarely built, in her late thirties but gallantly girlish. She splashed straight ahead and then turned around because she knew he was still looking at her. He was. He was looking at her with a very open look of liking her. He was like a clean spot on the messy corner of the spoke of P and Massachusetts and she liked his liking her. She suddenly remembered to thank him for his kindness.

"Thanks for sharing your cab," she called to him.

He called back, "Will you be hungry after you've looked at all those pictures?"

She knew she should say No.

"I'll be starved," she said.

That was the beginning.

"Do you believe in God?" Beverly Peck Gordon happened to ask Harvey Porter late that night as they sat drinking (coffee for her, bourbon for him) on yellow-covered armchairs in the little conversation arc of Beverly's big round room at the Watergate Hotel. She was already seeing her new friend as a kind of god himself because he had lived so long, felt his feelings so sharply, thought his thoughts so searchingly that he seemed to be a source of both good will and good judgment, characteristics that made him a lot more trustworthy than the bumbling busybody of a God her parents had occasionally invoked when she was a child and to whom she had prayed until she could no longer overlook wars and mongoloid babies, leukemia for sixteen-year-olds, burnings and starvings and the unconcern of comfortable people for the suffering of others, especially when the comfortable ones were often churchgoers of all faiths. No matter how philosophers tried to account for evil, Beverly could not accept it in good faith and, as for herself, she lived her life knowing that at any moment, no matter how decent she was (and she was *very* decent), she or anybody she loved and counted on could step out on the sidewalk and be shot, stabbed, struck by lightning, crushed by a passing truck or falling telephone pole, or picked up by secret police and sent to a camp to await extermination with all the other Jews, practicing or not, believing or not. She already knew that Harvey Porter would fight for her, would smuggle, hide, protect with his life every Jew he could find, which was, of course, more than her parents' God had done.

She already knew enough about Harvey Porter not to have hesitated when their midnight taxi U-turned on Virginia Avenue to cross the traffic island and backtrack to the taxi

entrance of the Watergate Hotel before asking very naturally if
he would like to come in for a cup of coffee. If it wasn't too
late. If he wasn't too tired. For it had been a long day and he
was not, after all, a young man, but on the other hand they
had been enjoying themselves so much that it seemed a
shame—at least, at the moment, to Beverly, who was enjoying
the feeling of being enjoyable—to stop. When it turned out
that the coffee shop was closed, Harvey Porter was not sorry to
go to the cocktail lounge, but Beverly—craving coffee—did
not hesitate to suggest her room, where there was both sitting
space and coffee-making apparatus.

By the time Beverly had made several cups of instant
coffee from the machine on the wall of her dressing room and
Harvey Porter had swallowed the last of the double bourbon-
on-the-rocks he had ordered from room service, these two
recent strangers of ethnic, geographic, and socio-economic
diversity had discovered—in a fortuitous mix of sympathy,
mirth, nostalgia, irony, and rue—that they were not, after all,
extremely distant branches on the Family Tree of Human-
kind. But, on the other hand, they were different.

By this time Beverly knew that Harvey Porter loved his
wife, Sally, who was fifty-one years old and who taught sixth
grade in a public school not far from their house, who took
good care of him and always tried to understand the deeper
needs of the people she had to deal with;

and Harvey Porter knew that Beverly loved her husband,
who was forty-one and generally successful in his business
though when it was up he always worried that it would go
down, and when it was down he always thought he was ruined;

and Beverly knew that Harvey Porter loved his daughters,

one of whom was married to a college professor and lived in Kansas City, while the other was married to a trucking executive and lived in Houston, and that the one in Kansas City had two children and the one in Houston had a job;

and Harvey Porter knew that Beverly would be damned if she would ever end up describing *her* daughter in terms of her daughter's husband's job;

and Beverly knew that Harvey Porter was not an irreversible sexist because he not only appreciated her point but took pains to let her know about his unstereotypical enjoyment of preparing summer suppers from the freshly picked produce of his back-yard vegetable garden, though he sometimes got mixed up and tried to make coleslaw from lettuce.

By the time Beverly had slung her shoeless feet over the arm of her yellow-covered chair and suggested that Harvey Porter at least loosen his necktie or take off his jacket or do *something* to free himself from what she considered the unbearable discomfort of sitting upright in buttoned-up business clothes, both these disparate people were finding themselves much more perceptive and articulate than they had been for a long time.

Beverly knew that Harvey Porter loved music by Berlioz and the prints of Currier and Ives and that he and his wife read serious books, which they discussed seriously during quiet evenings in twin wing chairs on either side of their fireplace;

and that he sometimes sat alone on the porch that stretched the length of his house and overlooked a broad lawn on which a wooden cross was once set afire by irate neighbors who wanted to burn into Harvey Porter's mind their dissatisfaction with his outspoken defense of a black family's right to own and live in a big, old, white house like his on the main street of the town;

and Harvey Porter knew that Beverly was a Marx Brothers freak who could break him up with her imitation of Harpo eating a cigar in A *Night at the Opera*, that once in extreme youth she had been the manager of a young tenor with operatic aspirations and that on a Mother's Day, not very many years before, she herself had written and performed at a Temple Sholom talent show a song that went:

> M   is for Momism
> O   is for Over-protected
> T   is for Trauma
>   (in childhood it's kind of expected)
> H   for Hostility
>   (which children vent in aggression)
> E   is for Ego
>   (dependent upon self-expression)
> R   is Right and Right I'll never be.
>
> Put me back together, I'm a mother
> All broke up by child psychology;

and that she believed, deep in her heart, that the Queen of England—when all the doors were shut and all the servants safely belowstairs—took off her shoes and her girdle and dropped the fancy accent.

Harvey Porter was grateful for the laughter that Beverly brought him. He had a neat wit himself, which he took out like a pair of ice skates he hadn't used for years. After one or two tries, holding on to the side rail, he found himself gliding smoothly, taking a few dips and curves, even moving into the center of the rink for an exhibitionistic twirl to impress his speedy little friend from the city. So by the time he had loosened his tie and laid his neatly folded suit jacket over the back of the yellow-covered couch, and Beverly was sitting on the floor with her legs crossed in one of the positions from her Tuesday-morning yoga class, they were both feeling inordinately alive and unusually unguarded. And Harvey Porter came to know that Beverly was feeling lately a little bit lost, a little bit dispensable, in a shrinking household which her son would be leaving for college in less than a year and from which her daughter was already beginning to reach away;

and that, though she was crazy about the painting of Ambrogio Lorenzetti, Piero della Francesca, Poussin, Degas, Cézanne, Seurat, Kirchner, and Richard Lindner, among others, she did not feel passionately committed to the study of art history and to the master's degree program in which she was currently enrolled, that—despite her many strong interests—she didn't feel committed, in truth, to anything, really, except the family which was growing away from her.

And Beverly came to know that Harvey Porter had suffered from disappointments and did not love life as much as he had years ago when he was a new, though no longer young, lawyer who thought he was riding on the crest of a wave of change;

that he regretted having been a too stern, perhaps too remote father, always more at ease with public issues than with personal problems, who had somehow failed to practice at home the liberalism he preached outside;

and that the turmoil of the sixties had left him defeated on both fronts, the wave of social change having subsided, receded, and disappeared, leaving the shoreline very much as it had been before, and his daughters having married conventionally, somewhat disappointingly, and become more remote than ever though they answered his letters and visited at least once a year, surely more for their mother's sake than his.

By the time Harvey Porter had carefully knocked the ashes out of his pipe into the china ashtray on the low table beside his chair and Beverly already knew that he had a formidable capacity for bourbon and he already knew that her right eye got small when she was tired, it did not seem so terribly forward, so out-of-the-way, so awfully gauche for Beverly to look into Harvey Porter's kind, intelligent, and only slightly bleary blue eyes and ask him out of the most sincere curiosity:

"Do you believe in God?"

Once, almost twenty years before, she had asked her boyfriend Peter Gordon the same important question. Peter was an energetic, impatient young man, who prided himself on being no phony-baloney. Beverly remembered his reply.

"Who's to know?" he had said. And Beverly had nodded her pretty little head as they ambled, hand in hand, beside one of the pretty little lakes in Central Park. The answer, like all Peter Gordon's answers in those days, had been all right with Beverly.

Harvey Porter thought before he spoke and it made him think he was slow. "I believe in the unknown," he said quietly.

"Do you think the unknown is knowable?"

"It has proved so in the past." He was immediately ashamed of himself for the sarcasm. Beverly laughed at his apology: "Don't worry. Just finish."

"There are things we may never learn scientifically, a shrinking island of what has not yet been discovered or proved. I think it will never entirely disappear."

"And what? That little island of mystery is God?"

"I suppose you could call it that. It doesn't interest me very much. I'm concerned not so much with the external as with the inside of things. The unconscious, if you like. Discovering God may be a matter of discovering what's inside oneself."

Now Beverly was slow.

"Do you and your wife go to church on Sundays?"

"Sally goes sometimes. We used to go as a family when the girls were small."

He smiled to himself and Beverly followed the smile into her version of his memory, where she saw two plain little girls in braids and starched dresses, plunked down on a hard pew between spare, solemn parents. The mother was a tight-faced woman with work-worn hands crossed on her narrow lap. The father was a young, handsome Lincolnesque rendition of Harvey Porter, straight as a pillar, with a hymnbook in his hands. If the girls got restless during the sermon of that laddery, black-clad Dimmesdale or Davidson up there on the pulpit, one finger raised by their father hushed them and they sat back like good little Puritans, among the rows of prim, sparse people in the plain, spare rows of pews on the hard wood floor of the square white church.

"Sally goes fairly regularly," Harvey Porter said, having returned from his memory before Beverly was finished with it. "I gave up that nonsense some time ago," he said.

"Oh yes. Yes," Beverly wanted to say. "Yes. I did, too." But, of course, she couldn't say it.

It was easy to give up churchgoing if you were a Gentile Protestant, a privileged citizen who could join any club or check in at any hotel without wondering if you were really wanted, would be really acceptable to the people already there, the people who did everything right or—better still, for them—knew that whatever they chose to do would automatically *become* right. It was easy, almost noble, if intellect or taste required a rejection of simpleminded piety, to drop a religion that made you automatically first class and opened doors to choice jobs, choice neighborhoods, choice recreational facilities, choice civic positions, and the homes of other first-class people. It was honorable to be an ex-Presbyterian or an ex-Episcopalian. But if you were a Jew and you wanted to give up "that nonsense," Beverly thought, you would be a rat deserting a sinking ship. So that, when she took four-year-old Allison to the hospital emergency room with a cut on her knee that might have needed stitches and, amid the little girl's crying and her own heart-pumping anxiety, somebody handed her a form to fill out, she could not bring herself—even then—to ignore the line that asked for *Religion (optional)*, but had to print in big, bold, gallant, foolish, proud letters: JEWISH.

The *tallith* (pronounced to rhyme with Hollis) is a prayer shawl. It is a striped rectangle of linen, cotton, silk, or wool—an unadulterated fabric, as prescribed by the commandments. Bar Mitzvah boys wear small silk ones with blue or violet stripes. As Beverly understood it—in the days when she tried to understand—the older and more pious a man becomes, the bigger and heavier becomes his *tallith*. In the days when she went to *shul* (pronounced to rhyme with school but meaning synagogue) with her grandfather, the old men—her grandfather's friends—wore *tallithim* (Hebrew plural form, as in cherubim, seraphim, and goyim) as big as tents, of linen heavy enough for tents and heavily striped in black on white. Sometimes the old men put the *tallithim* over their head as they swayed and prayed and they looked like tents or, from behind, to a little girl just coming in from the back, like a small herd of benign old elephants.

Beverly's grandfather, Old Man Rosen, who lived with his daughter Sadie as a stubbornly Old World member of a resolutely New World household, never missed a Saturday morning in *shul*. When Sadie Peck yelled at Beverly for not acting like a lady, Beverly ran to Grandpa Rosen for approval and comfort. When Sadie Peck yelled at her father for getting in the way, Grandpa Rosen took Beverly for a walk to the candy store. When Beverly could walk the distance, her Yiddish-speaking grandfather started towing her for what seemed like miles with his brown old hand tight around her wrist to the ancient synagogue that was already being squeezed off its narrow cobbled street by patchwork posted walls and five-story skyscrapers.

In Beverly's memory, her grandfather's *tallith* was woven with an encrustment of gold between the fabric proper and the fringe of tassels. The *tallith*, like the Torah cover with its gold-fringed epaulet, its beaten silver ears and breastplate, had been embroidered with love and reverence. In fact, when the rabbi and the cantor and the honored guests from the *bimah* marched around the *shul*, bringing the reverently, lovingly, punctiliously carried Torah down to the congregation, the men would reach out of their rows and take hold of a passing tassel—a tassel of the rabbi's *tallith* if they couldn't catch the Torah—and kiss it. Grandpa Rosen used to kiss the Torah, and when Beverly was with him, the only female on the floor of the synagogue, she used to do it, too.

Beverly's grandfather had a permanent seat in the third row on the right of the rabbi when he faced the congregation, on the left when he faced the Torah ark. It was Beverly's childpleasure to sit downstairs on the wooden bench that was worn to a shine by the daily rub, sunrise and sunset, of the sitting and rising pants seats of pious old Jews; to stand beside her stubble-chinned grandfather among his friends Mendel Grossman, Reb Yussel the slaughterer, Old Man Steinheimer, and Mr. Schwartz, the schoolteacher's father, who herded together in their heavy prayer shawls to worship and gossip and follow their own order of service, stubbornly out of line with the order of the young, black-bearded rabbi, a newcomer, an interloper they despised so heartily that, at the moment he closed his prayer book to begin his Sabbath sermon, the group turned on their worn heels and shambled in a body down the aisle, across the vestibule, and outside to the square, iron-railed balcony where they waited, arguing and offering each other snuff, until the sermon was over.

What they hated about the rabbi, these shuffling, muttering, fiercely devout old men who spoke in Yiddish and prayed in Hebrew, were his new ways, his by-the-book procedures (when by some other book than their old-country edition), the educated and impersonal tone of his voice, his youth, his dapper dress, his correct use of English. On one point, however, the rabbi and Old Man Rosen's friends agreed: that a woman, even if she was a little girl, had no business downstairs among the men. But there was nothing they could do about it. Isaac Rosen brought his granddaughter in and she stayed.

Often in the clean, odorless, carpeted temple where her

children had received their religious education and her husband occasionally went to pray (apart from his essential yearly appearances to honor his mother's memory on the anniversary of her death), Beverly was abruptly overtaken by a longing for the fierce mysteries of her grandfather's orthodoxy. Instead of the modern, decorous pulpit before her, she saw the *bimah* of the old *shul*—this musty, tarnished, frayed, and cluttered platform from which the detested new rabbi smiled with his false teeth. She remembered his black beard, his strong breath. She remembered his droning voice as he bent over his prayer book, bowing and swaying, *davening* into his beard, his service impossible to follow, his words unintelligible. She remembered the inchoate chant of the cantor with its muezzic sobbing that rose above the prayers of the congregants but never led them, chanted only with, over, under the muttering, mumbling, singing out, every man on his own time, every man in his own posture, the scraggle of old congregants turned this way and that, tented in their prayer shawls, leaning together, leaning apart, swaying, yawning and stretching as they finished a passage, her grandfather among them, holding her hand in his as she stood beside him smelling the snuff, the shoe polish, the gold watch and buttoned vest smell of poor old men in an old *shul*.

If she grew restless during the interminable sittings and standings, Beverly was free to go upstairs, by the curved wooden stairway in the vestibule to the gallery where Tanta Gittel, the dwarfish wigged wife of the custodian of the *shul*, a distant cousin of Old Man Rosen, sat with the other women behind a double layer of dotted swiss hanging from a low brass bar to curtain them from the view of the men. Tanta Gittel cackled at the sight of Beverly, hugged the child against her tightly bound breast that smelled of camphor and spices, gave her a dozen quick pats on the head, saying "Nice, nice," because she knew so little English, this jitter of a woman with a face oddly old and wrinkled against the chestnut-colored, center-parted wig that she had to wear as an Orthodox Jewish wife with a shaven head.

"Pssht!" the men hissed at Beverly, a round little girl with a pleasing smile and curious eyes. "Pssht!" She got furious looks from the *shamus*, Finkelstein the cripple, who handed out the prayer books and poked the Hebrew school boys when they got noisy. "Pssht!" Zimmer, the president of the congregation, turned around from his seat in the front row and glowered at her. But Beverly passed from upstairs to downstairs safe in her grandfather's insistence and rejoined the group of intransigents, who interrupted their praying only to whisper and hiss among themselves and occasionally fight with indignant neighbors about the rabbi's pronunciation of Hebrew or his lack of proper humility in the bowing of his head or the bending of his knee. Their criticism was never delicate. Their feelings were never subdued. "Go to hell!" Grandpa Rosen once growled at an antagonist during the prayers before the open Torah ark. Beverly was shocked and the little man thus addressed was rendered almost apoplectic by the sacrilege, but Grandpa Rosen jauntily stuck some snuff into his nose, safe from the wrath of God since he had said the words in English and English didn't count.

The *shul* was a place of mystery and excitement. When Beverly wanted to go to the bathroom, she had the marvelous opportunity to choose between two stairways, one of which led to an iodine-colored door and an ordinary washroom with basins and stalls with crinkly toilet paper that came out pre-cut in folded squares because Orthodox Jews were not allowed to tear on the Sabbath. But if she went down the other stairway, a mirror image on the other end of the vestibule, she would enter, through an identical iodine-colored door with an identical porcelain knob, an altogether different lavatory with a strong, burning smell and a row of three on-end bathtubs, each with a single plunger button that could be pushed to send water streaming down the tubs. Until she grew old enough to distinguish left from right, Beverly played this thrilling guessing game, always hoping to arrive at the more exciting door.

Downstairs also, beyond the classroom where the Hebrew school boys tormented their sighing teacher, was a broad row of shallow steps leading to the cavernous room where, after Sabbath services, after Bar Mitzvahs, after the happy holidays, a table as long as the room was lined down the middle with a row of platters on which were heaped chunks of honey cake and sponge cake and piles of brittle-capped *eir kichel* that Tanta Gittel baked every Friday of her life. The mannerless school boys grabbed for the cakes and paper cups of sweet kosher wine while the older men hefted down tiny glasses of schnapps with great gulps and shouts of *l'chaim*. Behind this gathering room, along a narrow passageway, was the apartment of Uncle Mordechai, the custodian, Grandpa Rosen's cousin, who looked like an eagle in a skullcap, and his wife Tanta Gittel, who spent her life outside the gallery running from sink to icebox to stove to table, her wig slipping, her eyeglasses jiggling, and her mouth never stopping.

"A terrible gossip," Beverly heard people complain about Tanta Gittel. "A two-faced troublemaker." But Beverly liked the old lady, almost as small as she, whose dry old hands flew as she fussed over the *schoene maidele* and fed her cookies in the dazzlingly clean basement kitchen where there was always a bowl of polished wax fruit on a crocheted or embroidered tablecloth. "Eat, eat!" the old lady would cry, rubbing at the sweetness of Beverly's fat arms, and the next minute would contort her wizened face to squawk in harsh Yiddish at her woebegone, clipped-winged husband.

"She cares only about her children," adjudged Beverly's mother, Sadie Peck, who not only kept far away from the synagogue but even cooked forbidden bacon sometimes when the old man was out of the house. Tanta Gittel had been married at least once more than once and the focus of the strife in the shiningly clean apartment under the *shul* was a tug of Uncle Mordechai's children against hers. But Beverly's most salient memory was of hopping little Tanta Gittel leading her through the apartment and down a linoleum-lined hall with latticed doors along one wall and into the room of the *mikvah*, the swimming pool with steps leading deep down, the ritual bath in which pious women cleansed themselves. Beverly begged to "go in" but Tanta Gittel cackled and kissed her and hurried her back to the warm, odoriferous kitchen where lamb had been baking since before Friday sundown in preparation for the meal at sundown of the Sabbath.

Over thirty years later, when Tanta Gittel's children and Uncle Mordechai's children had long since buried the hatchet if indeed they were not buried themselves, Beverly thought that going back to religion might help to lighten the terrible black weight of her depression. She attended services of which all the words were clear to her, all the meanings carefully explained in the text and in the accompanying sermons that were meant to be relevant to the present day as well as the ancient liturgy. Bent with despair, corrugated with dread,

Beverly allowed herself to be taken on one, two, three, four Friday nights to one, two, three, four temples within reasonable traveling distance and none of them did her any good. When the words were written in plain English, she no longer cared about them. She had loved the magic and the magic was gone. The old synagogues were crumbling and the pale, bearded zealots who still clung to orthodoxy were as foreign to her as the Amish, the Hare Krishnas. Yet the respectable, acceptable genteel temples of suburban America seemed cold and bloodless. Her grandfather, she knew, would not have set foot in these modish, sterilized temples with well-behaved congregations that prayed in unison. "What?" Grandpa Rosen would yell in his East European accent. "A *shul* with no *yarmulkes?* They don't cover their heads? No *tallithim?* They sit with the women?" The old man would spit on the sidewalk. "This is not a *shul*. This is a church. These people are *goyim*." Beverly, sick of soul, had to look elsewhere for the healing balm. Her religion did not sustain her.

Her religion did not sustain her but there was no question of changing it, denying it, or forgetting about it.

Her religion did not sustain her, but, on the other hand, no matter how heavy her depression or how light her euphoria, she could never in all the highs and lows of her life stop feeling it her perverse, unlooked-for, grave, express, comic, tragic, infuriating, and absolutely inescapable duty to sustain her religion.

So when the distinguished Gentile Harvey Porter shrugged off his Presbyterian past, saying, "I gave up that nonsense some time ago," Beverly could understand and even envy him. She envied the hands-off past of his parents and

their parents, his church, his fellow Presbyterians who probably felt themselves so truly chosen that one or two members
who unaccountably wished to forfeit the benefits of belonging
were no great loss to the flock, but actually a boon to those
who stayed and had that much more bounty to divvy up. She
understood the ease with which he could detach himself. Harvey Porter as a boy in the blanched country church of his
parents had never been titillated by the mysteries of Hebrew or
Latin, had not been tantalized by twin curving stairways, fonts
of holy water, an exotic rabbi, an exalted priest, swirling black
robes, a gloried Torah enthroned in its ark, the Sacred Heart,
the Lion of Judah, the crucifix, the body, the blood, the *mikvah*.

Instead of curtained darkness, Harvey Porter had seen the
light. The plain talk, the bare walls, the spare white church
with its modest steeple. His senses had not been penetrated,
transported, and enthralled by early initiation into a voluptu-
ous religion.

It was easy for him to be a man of reason.

Beverly thought this without bitterness.

The next morning when she saw the arm, a reaching
hand stretched upward, glovelike, from a base below the elbow, she slowed up only to check the printed card on the stand
and give herself the customary mental pat for having recognized it as the work of Picasso. She stopped only to examine
the works that stopped her. Otherwise, she kept moving, enjoying the sun, the plants, the soft carpet, the cool sophistica-
tion of the Hirshhorn Museum that was set—startling in its
circular modernity—among the somber, formidable, conform-
ing Greco-Colonial buildings of the Smithsonian Institution

along the Mall between the Capitol and the Washington Monument. Beverly felt serenely at home among the cultivated amenities of the Hirshhorn, where even the sleek black chairs were comfortable and sedulously placed in sunlit space among living plants to swivel noiselessly toward a dramatic view out, out over Washington or in across the lovely center court to see the gallery meeting itself on the other side. She moved slowly, enjoying an atmosphere that was as light and dry as good French perfume, enjoying interior warmth that was more satisfying because of the cold beyond the transparent wall, enjoying the new art she had begun to appreciate since her return to school. And then she stopped. A nick of memory stopped her. She went back to look at the Picasso hand.

Passing , she read a sign on the wall between the sculpture and the paintings:

IN THE MUSEUM . . .
PLEASE . . . MUSE, CONVERSE, SMOKE,
STUDY, STROLL, TOUCH, ENJOY, LITTER,
RELAX, EAT, LOOK, LEARN . . .

Smoky blue X's ruled out the Don'ts. But there were more Do's and Beverly liked that. It was, she thought in passing, a hell of a good way to run a museum . . .

There was a number on the arm.

On the inside of the forearm of Picasso's bronze sculpture titled *The Arm*, which stood like a black glove on an iron stem, was scratched, casually, it seemed, a number. 15-3-59. That was what Beverly had come back to see.

She thought it was a mistake. A catalogue number penciled on in a warehouse. For shipment. They had forgotten to erase it.

She thought some rotten kid had scratched it on. The only piece of graffiti in the whole place.

She thought, *Of course, Picasso intended it.* Picasso the war-hater. Picasso the humanist.

Then she thought, *Oh my God. It's the date he finished it. I'm really getting paranoid.*

Beverly had seen numbers on arms many times since the Bar Mitzvah Depression had forcefully opened her eyes to the fact that life was not a bowl of cherries. One hot Sunday morning, in one of her desperate attempts to regain old magic, she and Peter and Sandy and Allison had visited the lower East Side of Manhattan, that redolent corner of Jewdom where her mother's parents had lived out the chaos of their first years in the New World, which was still a poor neighborhood (though Yiddish was giving way to Spanish) but which was also a newly fashionable discount shopping area as well as a fairly self-conscious center for the purveyance of Jewish nostalgia. Walking in the street because the sidewalks were crowded with shoppers pawing merchandise on the outdoor tables and merchants standing over them to catch the shoplifters and others sitting around in folding chairs with skin like bagel dough and sweat under their sleeves; walking in the street, which was also crowded with shoppers and tourists and locals carrying noisy transistor radios, all in the middle of the road because the gutters were awash with newspapers and soda cans and other more colorful garbage; walking and smelling the sour pickles and onion rolls, eating kosher franks and potato knishes, Sandy smiling with condescension when Peter pointed out the

tenement where his great-aunt Ethel used to live and Allison
awed by the Chasidic hardware man with his curling *payis* and
black felt hat under which he sweated like a melting candle,
Beverly found the outing pleasant enough with Peter and the
children close enough around her to hold off the Furies of her
depression. They went into a cluttered tube of a store on Orchard Street. Allison wanted a pair of pantyhose and Sandy
needed athletic socks for back-to-school and maybe Peter
could use some jockey shorts (Beverly hated his shapeless box-
ers). Buying this and that, they talked about this and that with
the friendly proprietor who was squeezed behind the counter,
a small man with a face like a razor blade, but dreamy-eyed,
and wearing a skullcap as most Orchard Street merchants did.
Just for Beverly, because she had such a nice, big smile, the
proprietor ripped open a fresh cellophane package, no obliga-
tion, to show Allison that the pantyhose was a very pretty pink
on the skin. He held the pantyhose out to them, over the
counter in his outstretched arms as he might have held the
limp body of a thin, dead child, and Beverly saw the number.

The children were embarrassed by her carrying on. Peter
gave her his handkerchief. "Don't cry for me." The proprietor
comforted her. "I am a lucky man. I'm here in this country."
The man had blessings to count: a good wife, good children
getting a good education. He made a living in his store. Every
day he thanked God. "The past is past," he said. But he still
carried the number, like a six-figure laundry mark tattooed
into his forearm.

Beverly had seen the arm of a fellow guest at a hotel in
San Juan. ("A change of scene," the doctor had told Peter
when he could find nothing physically wrong with her.) The
woman was not much older than Beverly. She was a zesty

redhead who had a fruit business in Montreal. The numbers ran lengthwise a few inches above the wrist. "It taught me to grab," she told Beverly as they sat swishing their feet in a swimming pool on a terrace overlooking the Caribbean Sea. "To grab for every day I wake up to and squeeze the life out of it."

And once when she was trying a new hairdresser in a swanky city shop. ("Come, I'll go with you," her friend Martha had said. "We'll get a facial and then we'll get our hair styled. You'll feel a lot better.") Inches in front of her eyes was the number—light blue this time—across the meaty arm of the woman who was washing her hair. "I could have it taken off," she told Beverly. "It's a small operation, plenty of people do it. But not me. I don't want to forget. Let them all see."

"I gave up that nonsense some time ago." In the Hirshhorn Museum, Beverly turned from the haunting arm to a dream picture of Harvey Porter's calm and calming face. She thought she would like to tell him, someday, about the numbers. And then she thought she should spare him, having an inkling already of how much it would hurt him. But this was a morning that had not happened yet, a morning still several hours away, when Beverly would be looking forward to a late lunch and a slow afternoon in the company of her new companion. On the night before, in the round room of the Watergate Hotel, it was impossible to know that the next morning would bring her to the arm or that the night of the morning after would bring her closer to Harvey Porter than she had ever been to any other man and that she would ask him, holding his hands, holding his face in her eyes, wanting to hold him forever, speaking with more tenderness than she had ever before found in herself:

"Do I compensate for any of the disappointments in your life?"

and he would kiss her eyes and hold her again apart from him, so that he could frame her in his memory. "Having known you," he would say, "will nourish me for the rest of my life."

But on this night, still the night before, and only the first night of the first day they had spent together, Beverly, in stocking feet, walked Harvey Porter to the door of her room. They shook hands.

"Shall we meet tomorrow?" His eyes were as ardent as a boy's and Beverly was surprised to see that he was not quite, not only, a kind old fellow passing the time.

"Yes," she said. Without hesitation.

CHAPTER 3 _____

Still, she was surprised when he kissed her.

He had been playing her husband's advocate for most of the afternoon.

Downtown Washington was all torn up with patches of reconstruction, and the streets that were not clotted with excavations, sandpiles, pipes, planks, platforms, and working hardhats were clogged with traffic and none too clean. But yesterday's rain had opened up the sky and an indulgent October sun smiled through it, inviting walking. Harvey Porter and Beverly accepted with pleasure.

They walked on Independence Avenue toward the still-green park of the Washington Monument, around which

53

groups of tourists and schoolchildren were deployed and which Harvey Porter saw as a giant phallic symbol of authoritative strength while Beverly saw it more as an upraised industrialistic middle finger giving an "Up yours" to the underprivileged of the world. At Fourteenth Street they turned toward Pennsylvania Avenue and the White House—behind its fences and gates and sentry houses—which Harvey Porter extolled as the home of the free and the brave while Beverly pronounced it the scene of the crime. However, by the time they were walking across the diameter of Lafayette Square, the White House comings and goings were reduced to toy sentries stopping toy cars on a felt turf with lollipop trees. And as they lolled along H Street in the lavish sunlight that glanced off the creamy walls of George Washington University, Harvey Porter and Beverly were no longer aware of buildings and monuments.

Harvey Porter was a very acceptable closeup. He had jettisoned his briefcase at a hotel stop on his way to the Hirshhorn from his completed contract. He had exchanged his suit jacket for a light blue sweater—one hundred percent virgin wool, Beverly was sure. He was carrying his topcoat over his arm and he looked healthy, color in his face, light in his eyes.

"I think I know how Peter feels," he said as they stopped for a red light on the corner of New Hampshire Avenue. "When a man reaches his forties, he begins to feel that he hasn't used his life as well as he ought."

Beverly did not move when the light changed. "I was never a demanding wife. He can't blame me."

"It isn't a question of blame. A woman needs to be especially compassionate."

"Maybe," Beverly said, "she needs to be a saint."

The lights were dimming in the House of Gordon and had been dimming gradually over the last three years, ever since the curtain had fallen on the long-run domestic comedy in which Peter and Beverly were the romantic leads and Sandy and Allison the juvenile supporting characters.

Despite the small cast and the single setting, it had not been a low-budget production; that was part of the reason for its closing. Peter—who was producer as well as leading man—continually complained that the costs were outrunning the profits. But the major cause for the discontinuation of performances was a script problem between the leading lady and the director, who was Peter also.

Beverly Peck Gordon, the star, was no longer satisfied with the subject or style of the play. The original lighthearted frolic was no longer suited to her dramatic talents, which had perforce expanded since she was first cast as an ingenue back in the fifties and which had certainly gained strength with the melodramas and political satires that had been added to the repertory as occasional *divertissements* during the sixties. Beverly wanted a stronger role and also a stronger voice in company policy. The juveniles, too, were discontented: they showed their boredom with the scenario by slipping out of character, often disrupting performances and sometimes refusing to appear onstage at all, but showing up in the audience and booing the leading players.

Peter Gordon, however, would not hear the word "change." The investment was his. The playhouse was his. The leading lady—though she had become excitable, uncompromising, caustic, scornful, and a lot heavier both literally and figuratively since she took over the part—was also his. And he was determined to keep things that way.

Of course, Beverly couldn't tell the whole story. She could not be disloyal to her husband. Besides, Harvey seemed to feel sorrier for Peter than he did for her. He made her feel that she was kicking a man who was down.

When Harvey Porter was forty years old, some fifteen years before he described the situation to Beverly Gordon, he decided that he could not bear to spend one more day of his life in an overcrowded, overheated classroom, teaching American history to a group of unresponsive, overprivileged, and overcharged eighth-graders in a New Haven private school where the clawlike headmaster paid substandard salaries to teachers like Harvey Porter, who were at his mercy because they had been unwilling to put up with the rigmarole of the "education" courses required at teachers colleges for public school teaching accreditation. Besides, thought Harvey Porter, who had served stateside during World War II: I have lived long enough as a bystander. I would rather make American history than teach it.

And so he had thought about quitting, changing, getting away, making a new start. And the more he thought, the angrier he felt with himself for only thinking, and as he became angrier with himself, he became sullen in his house and his garden withered and his wife shrank away from him and his daughters got up from the supper table and went straight to their room. At first, Sally tried to comfort him, but he would take no comfort. Then she began to lose patience with a man who seemed to love his own misery. She recognized her dissatisfaction with a man who did nothing but moon around the house with last week's newspaper, not even walking the dog unless he was told to do it, and while Sally was not a forward woman, never easy in sexual conduct, she became aware of how much time elapsed between the nights when her husband came into her bed. As Harvey Porter's misery curled tighter and his anger clawed deeper, the sorrier he felt for Sally and the guiltier for the worn-out living-room rug and the girls' homemade dresses, the refrigerator that dripped, the porch glider that was held together with rope. The guiltier he felt, the more he tried to make it up to Sally by helping with the washing and waxing, and the more housework he did, the less she liked him for it, until she started to shoo him out of the kitchen when she was cooking and off the porch when she was sweeping. In the end he had managed to distribute his plenteous anger (as for years he had done with his insufficient pay) among all the members of his family and his girls were already in trouble (though he didn't know it yet) and Sally had inhaled her own vapors of guilt and resentment until she was so inflated that she spewed them out on him, letting him know that she had made a mistake to marry a man so weak and vacillating that he could neither rise to his job nor leave it for a better one, letting him know he was a disappointment to her and a liability to his daughters. Feeling contemptible, contaminating, wronged, and culpable, Harvey packed up and left home one night and stayed with his brother in Boston for three weeks until Sally came to beg him for the girls' sake and for hers to come back. She had been sitting at her kitchen table peeling and peeling at the sticky layers of their troubles, and she knew she wanted Harvey back but only if he'd quit his job so he could feel like a man again.

Furthermore—Harvey Porter pointed out to Beverly as they walked in Georgetown past the health-food stores and bookshops on M Street—Sally had proved her strength and fealty by bringing her own accreditation up to date and taking up a teaching career to help put her husband through law school.

"So you see," Harvey Porter said, "I'm not entirely unacquainted with liberated women."

"Since then," he said, "our marriage has been a good one."

"I sympathize with Peter," he said. "You mustn't let those layers accumulate."

And yet, he telephoned his home, at four-thirty that afternoon, having calculated almost to the minute when she would be getting back from school, to tell Sally that business was going to keep him in Washington another day.

Beverly intended to stay just one night in Washington, which would give her two days away and only one dinner missed. Happily eating her lunch from a tray at a window table in the second-floor public cafeteria in the Department of Transportation Building, she could look out at the Hirshhorn with its giant back-yard sandbox studded with sculptures and in at Harvey Porter, sitting opposite her, happily eating his lunch from a proper place setting—fork, knife, coffee spoon, napkin—that he had neatly arranged after taking his tray to a service cart across the room. Beverly had paid for their lunch. First to the cash register, she had both trays added up so that when Harvey Porter came up behind her, the cashier wouldn't take his money.

"You shouldn't have done that," he said as they stood with their trays, eying the busy tables. "I'm on an expense account."

"For four dollars and seventy-five cents I can be a sport."

An unoccupied window table drew them without a word. "Besides, I'm not on your expense account and you signed for both of us last night."

She watched him fooling around with his plates and silverware. "You want a napkin ring? Could I get you a crystal goblet?" She wouldn't let him take her tray. "I eat like the workers," she said.

Harvey Porter thought she was very funny. She wouldn't let him get away with anything: "I'm surprised that an upstanding citizen like you, a Mayflower man and all, would include a picked-up lady on his expense account."

Harvey Porter confessed still greater sins. "I look for loopholes when I do my income tax." Beverly was sorry to hear it. She wanted him pure.

His business in Washington was done. He had settled his case, negotiated the contract so that neither party was triumphant and neither distressed. A check for his fee would arrive in the mail in a week or so in his little upstairs office on Main Street in Waddingford, Connecticut. There would be other cases, most of them much like this one, to be settled with good sense, with reasonable compromise. Settled out of court. It was almost a slogan for his life since he had given up fighting.

On her part, Beverly, too, had got what she came for. She had seen the nineteenth-century paintings. She had seen the Hirshhorn Museum. She had had a day off and a good though short night's sleep. As a bonus, a garnish, whipped cream on the sundae, she had enjoyed the company of a very courtly man, with humor, intelligence, a kind heart, and the cleanest fingernails she had ever seen. Her little trip was a great success. If she took the three-o'clock shuttle to LaGuardia Airport, she could even be home in time to cook the dinner.

"Will you stay another night?" Harvey Porter asked her.

Of course she couldn't.

For one thing, she had no household help. It was over a year since she tearfully dismissed Auntie Carrie after almost nine years of close association, explaining that it was impossible for her, Beverly, to go on exploiting her, Carrie, and Auntie Carrie had reasonably protested: "But honey, it's easy here. Ain't noplace I'm going to get work without busting my ass for less pay." Auntie Carrie, who had lived longer and harder than Beverly and had spent her adult life doting on a gambling husband, sat down in the half-vacuumed dining ell and spelled it out on the extendible dining table. "Girl," she said, "you'll be on the right side of your conscience and I'll be up shit's creek." Auntie Carrie's torchy style of advice had never appealed to Beverly but her uncalculated solicitude had been a steady hand held out through hard times and, furthermore, Beverly had also helped to ease Carrie out of a few pinches, so between them there was a closeness that smugly skirted the boundaries of master-servant propriety. Carrie said, "Pete giving you grief about money, that's something I understand. You know I'd still help you out when I could." So Beverly prevailed by shortening Carrie's hours and raising her hourly pay so that she could take a course in baby nursing, and soon Auntie Carrie was in such demand as a baby nurse that she was subcontracting her jobs and had anted her husband into a higher stake game. She and Beverly still kept in touch though, and Auntie Carrie never forgot, on Sandy's and Allison's birthday, to send a flowery birthday card with a dollar bill folded inside with the message. Her professional success, however, left Beverly with a big split-level house to clean, and by asking help from Sandy, Allison, and Peter (who usually bought himself off) she arrived not so much at having a clean house to live in as at being able to share the responsibility for the mess.

So there would be nobody home to cook dinner that night. On the other hand, there was food in the freezer and there was Sandy, who at seventeen might be depended upon to heat a TV turkey dinner without blowing up the kitchen, and there was Allison, who at fifteen should be capable of laying out a couple of forks and cleaning up afterwards. So it might not be totally impossible for two advanced adolescents to manage dinner without their absent mother's having to turn herself in for child abuse. Because, on the other hand, there was no way to know whether Peter would be home or not, and if he was home, whether he would eat with them or not, and if he ate with them, whether or not he would have a word to say, probably not. So, all in all, since she had no classes that week and no meetings of her women's Consciousness-Raising group and had gradually over the past few years given up bridge and the Sisterhood, hair sets, ladies' lunches, and volunteer work at the public school library and had no clothes to shop for and no rooms to redecorate, there really was not very much for Beverly to go home to.

She looked at the gray-haired gentleman sitting across from her at the white Formica-topped cafeteria table in a government building with functions she had never thought about. There was gray in her hair, too, though it didn't show up in the sun-bleached windblown mix of light and darker brown. Beverly Gordon knew that for all her mouth and stride, she was a woman who never took chances. She was close to forty and telling herself she had to hurry home. At the first thought of a change of plan, a tremor shot through her center.

> *Ladybug, Ladybug,*
> *Fly away home!*
> *Your house is on fire,*
> *Your children will burn.*

Yet she knew that the minute she opened her front door and hung up her coat on the quilted closet hanger and walked across the carpeted hall and up the half-stairway to the master bedroom with the initialed spread she had, before leaving just one morning ago, carefully laid over the king-sized bed, she would ask herself why she had come back so soon, what was she hurrying home for? Sandy would be in his room with stereo records and college catalogues, reluctant to break the magic of his privacy. Allison would be on one of her everlasting phone calls and would probably shut her bedroom door when she heard Beverly's footsteps. When Peter got home he would kiss her roundly and ask "How was your quest for culture?" but he wouldn't wait for an answer.

But there's no place else to go, was the answer Beverly always gave to the question of going home. Even when the kids were in camp and Peter was out of town. Now she had a place to stay a little longer and someone to stay with, whose company she enjoyed and, even better, who enjoyed hers and who happened to be—although he was a lot older than she—a man; and somehow (Beverly heard the ripple of a tiny giggle in the back of her head) it was especially agreeable (Women's Movement notwithstanding) to stay someplace in the company of an agreeable man. For in the suburbs where Beverly came from, male society on weekdays was a rare treat. In the suburbs, where Beverly came from, all the men left town on the buses that brought the housemaids in. The few men left around were those that women either gave orders to or took directions from. Even at weekend parties, where men were plentifully available, Beverly had found that it was almost impossible to be friendly without flirting or responsive without being on guard. Recently, since her entrance into the arena of Women's Rights, she had been accused by men (her husband prominently included) of being opinionated, argumentative, tactless, and overly sensitive, so she had spent a good deal of her time among men trying to keep from making a nuisance of herself. Therefore, she was particularly happy in the company of a man like Harvey Porter who was man enough to take a woman straight. She knew she could say anything—playfully, seriously, irreverent, irrelevant—and Harvey Porter would listen and hear her, not confusing her voice with voices of his past from which he had to hide or defend himself or which he needed to outshout.

So when they were walking in Georgetown, looking in the windows of the kind of stores that the hedonistic young like to spend their money in, Beverly, too, stopped in a drugstore near the corner of Wisconsin Avenue to phone Peter's office and tell his secretary to tell Peter when he got in that she wouldn't be home until tomorrow night. Then she called her house where there was, of course, nobody home, so she had to wait till later to tell the kids to make their own dinner or—if worst came to worst—to order something from the Chinese take-out.

There had to be other people on M Street in midafter-noon on a warm October day. There had to be college kids from the two universities, tourists, local shoppers, residents. They were not on a clear screen: Harvey Porter and Beverly. Their adventure was taking place on changing ground, their space defined by the row of shops, their lighting provided by the sunny sky, their scene further set by a background of characteristic noise and movement: doors shut, brakes jammed, horns tooted, people called, coins dropped, packages passed from hand to hand. Sidesteppings. Casual profanities. A grocer's delivery boy must have parked his bike alongside the curb. The cash register must have jingled behind the open door of the Souvlaki & Pizza Palace. And all these integrated sights and sounds were apprehended through the mistiest of filters and, for all Harvey Porter cared at that point of time, might have risen from the earth and sailed slowly down the Potomac River, as out of sight and mind as the buildings and monuments of the federal government. Harvey Porter's focus—which had grown more and more elastic over the past ten years—was tightly contracted on the very real, very present experience of this vibrant, vulnerable person he was with who challenged his upbringing, questioned his ideals, laughed at him, and took him so seriously that he had to be as careful with his words as if he were pleading a case in court.

They drifted past a fashionable china shop.

"I have friends whose houses look just like this window display."

"They must be very attractive houses."

"I guess they are—if you like rooms like show windows and don't mind not touching things."

Harvey Porter almost took her arm to cross the street and reminded himself not to. "My parents were like that," he said. "But it wasn't because their furniture was new and expensive. It was because it was old and rickety."

"You weren't a rich kid?"

"No. We were barely comfortable. My grandfather and his oldest son, my Uncle John, mismanaged the family fortune. My father, who was much younger, had to leave college and take a job with the railroad."

Beverly stopped short to study the flavor list in the window of the Ice Cream Factory. "My parents kept plastic over everything—even the breakfast cereal, to keep it fresh." She tapped Harvey Porter's wrist. "Cinnamon pumpkin. Is that one flavor or two?"

"I don't know," he said judiciously. "Want some?"

In a gift shop up Wisconsin Avenue, Beverly stood helplessly among pennants and belt buckles and paperweights with images of the capital's leading tourist attractions.

Harvey Porter, across the aisle and toward the back, hefted a succulent-looking wax apple that made him think of Snow White's stepmother and brought to Beverly's mind, when she saw it, a flash of Tanta Gittel's kitchen. "I don't like candles," she called to him. "They just melt away."

"Kids seem to like them," he said as Beverly joined him. "My daughters used to keep extensive collections on their bookshelves. Some of these are scented." He smelled the apple and held it out to her.

Beverly went around the counter and picked up a Tootsie Roll candle that smelled something like chocolate. An odorless teddy bear. A giant crayon. A lovely green frog with red spots. A tall white ghost that smelled ridiculously of mint. A silly purple tulip that smelled of lavender. She gave it to Harvey Porter, who cupped it between his palms and ran his fingers over the smoothly lipped ridges. He smelled it again and passed it back to her. "It's like the wine we had last night," he said. "The aroma improves with handling." Beverly bought the tulip for Allison. And then, even more impractically, she bought an eyeball paperweight for Sandy.

And yet

when she emerged from the phone booth, having at last reached her children, it was Harvey Porter who dryly observed, "Your husband seems to take very good care of you."

Beverly didn't want to tell him about the stocks she'd got on her twenty-first birthday. "You're right," she said. "Here I am living like a queen on his hard-earned money. You're absolutely right."

He saw that he had hurt her and he was sorry. He touched her shoulder. "It's interesting to me," he said as they went out and walked on, "that a woman of your acuity and energy— not to mention convictions—doesn't have a career of her own."

"You mean an income," Beverly said.
"You mean a degree of financial independence," she said.
"I started out ambitious," she said.

High adventure was out of style in the fifties, so Beverly went downtown to Manhattan to seek her fortune along with likelier candidates who had big white teeth, freckled noses, influential fathers, and silver spoons in their hope chests. Beverly, who didn't even know how to make her eyelashes look longer, had to open her own doors. She was a cute little Jewish girl of twenty and she pushed hard, but the other side of the door was always a disappointment.

She thought she'd like to be a newspaper reporter:
"We have a clerk-typist opening in retail advertising."
"Could I work my way up?"
"Sure. If you learn stenography, you can get to be a secretary."

She thought she'd go into advertising:
"We need somebody to walk the art director's dogs."
"Would you like to see my transcript? My honorary keys? My portfolio of extracurricular activities? My diploma with the *magna cum laude?*"
"How do you feel about German shepherds?"

So she thought she'd try public relations:
"Two-man office. Plenty of opportunity."
"You mean I could learn the business?"
"Sure, honey. You could start tonight. Drinks at my place?"

Beverly could still, in the cells of her memory, smell the Apple Blossom eau de cologne on the woman in the employment agency who looked at her with unseeing eyes and said,

"Tell me something about yourself."

"What could I tell her"—Beverly rhetorically asked Harvey Porter over Cokes in the Georgetown Inn coffee shop—"to crack that glaze in her eyes? How could I let her know I was special? *I have a good head on my shoulders. I could recite the Prologue to* Evangeline *when I was six. I was in the first co-ed class of the Bronx High School of Science.*

"Should I tell her I have a kind heart? I've been job-hunting since the day after college and my mother is ready to throw me out of the house? My father is telling his customers I should have gone to Katharine Gibbs? My high school boyfriend has just got engaged to a girl from Scarsdale? She's going to be married to a doctor and here I am in this hot, sweat-smelling office probably smelling slightly sweaty myself, trying to get you to see that I'm the smartest, hardest-working, most likely to succeed girl on my block, which is a block as big as the Bronx?"

But Beverly was genteel as her mother had taught her to be, and ultimately the Apple Blossom woman gave her a little pink card to introduce her to the editor of a fashion magazine. Beverly was not the height of fashion, but the little pink card said "careful screening" and it gave her confidence that she could handle the job, which was answering reader mail at a salary as low as the fashion was high.

The offices of *Debutante* looked like a beehive with desks in the cells, and all the worker bees were size-seven women with sheath dresses and slick hair and cheekbones as shiny and sharp as their fingernails. In her dun-colored suit, heavy shoulder bag, and Cuban-heeled shoes, Beverly felt like a blundering horsefly.

And worse when she met the Queen Bee.

Isobel Cotter was the editor. "She was"—Beverly explained to Harvey Porter—"just like all the other women executives in those days when nice women knew their place. They were not nice women. They ate their drones for breakfast and spat them out in time for lunch. And they had another thing in common: they all wore hats. All day long. It was a symbol of power, but I didn't know. Somebody led me to the throne room with Danish modern and carpeting and plants and blowups on the wall and there was Isobel Cotter in a hat, so I thought she was about to leave.

"It was a big hat with feathers. I thought I was keeping her from an important date.

"So I sat on the edge of my chair and answered her in short, quick sentences. I was ready to grab my portfolio and run. Her telephone started to ring while she was talking to me and I said, 'Go ahead, answer it. Don't worry about me.'

"My mother always taught me to be considerate of my elders.

"So she picked up the phone and then she slammed it down again. 'I don't answer my phone,' she said. 'My secretary answers my phone.' I could tell I was making her very nervous. I said, 'I'm sorry. I didn't know.' I said, 'I was only worrying about you.'

"She looked at me as if she just realized she was dealing with a lizard. 'You don't have to worry about me,' she said. She hated lizards.

"I fell all over myself apologizing and finally I explained the whole thing. 'I know you're in a hurry,' I said, 'because you've got your hat on.' "

Beverly thought the story was very funny but Harvey Porter felt sorry for the girl at the interview. "Did you ever find a job?" he wanted to know. They were walking hard and uphill toward Dumbarton Oaks, Beverly refusing every opportunity to admit she was tired and take a rest.

"Of course I got a job," she said, puffing. "Lots of jobs."

Mrs. Rhame called in sick.

Beverly said she was terribly sorry, but she was really glad to have a chance to show her stuff to Mr. Friedman. Mr. Friedman was the advertising director. Mrs. Rhame was his secretary. Beverly was Mrs. Rhame's assistant. A friend in high places was just what she needed.

Beverly had already learned that alacrity, diligence, competence, and good behavior were not enough. The union representative, a tubby man with a pinkie ring, had already told her to cut out the funny business. The coming in early. The staying late. The writing sales letters for salemen who should be writing their own. Beverly was making it tough for the other girls, the union representative said. Besides, it wouldn't do her any good. There was a regular schedule for raises, whether she worked hard or not.

"But I want to get into the newsroom."

"News you don't get into from advertising."

"How about sales promotion?"

"Listen. After a while you could discreetly apply to sell classified ads over the telephone. You'd like it there. Those girls make good money."

Beverly promised to cut out the funny stuff.

But the day Mrs. Rhame called, choking in her head cold, Beverly was determined to give her all. Mrs. Rhame started to tell her how to answer Mr. Friedman's telephone and how to take his dictation, but right in the middle her carburetor flooded and she had to hang up and run for a decongestant. Beverly, sitting importantly at the secretary's desk, decided that she would conduct herself in cool imitation of Mrs. Rhame, who was a classy older woman of thirty.

She was sitting there coolly at nine-forty when Mr. Friedman strode by her into his office and rang the buzzer.

Beverly rushed in with a steno pad.

"Morning, Miss Rhame," Mr. Friedman said.

"No, no. It's I. Beverly Peck. Mrs. Rhame is out sick."

Mr. Friedman was a big, bald man who wore shirts with his initials on the pockets. He jerked his jaw toward Beverly and said, "Take my coat, will you?"

Mrs. Rhame hadn't mentioned coats. Mr. Friedman's was a camel's-hair coat with a belt in the back. Beverly quickly sized him up and walked around behind him. She didn't know what to do with the pad and pencils or whether to get a hanger first. When she got everything settled, she stood up on her toes and found she couldn't get the coat off his shoulders. She stared mournfully at the thick hedge of hair between Mr. Friedman's camel's-hair collar and his stony skull. Eventually, he swung around and snatched the hanger and hung up his own coat.

Beverly was expected to keep the venetian blinds in an even line along Mr. Friedman's window walls. She was expected to keep his lead-weighted pitcher filled with ice water. She was expected to keep his pencils sharp and to call him Sir and to take a letter.

But she didn't write fast enough.

Soon Mr. Friedman got tired of repeating sentences. He

pressed his buzzer and asked to borrow the secretary of the retail advertising manager. It was nine-forty-eight.

Beverly Peck Gordon, who had not sought a promotion in eighteen years, and Harvey Porter, who supported himself, were collapsed on a bench in the cooling sunlight that slanted across the lawns of Dumbarton Park.

"My career made a housewife's lot look pretty good."

"And of course you loved Peter," he reminded her.

She was startled. "Of course I did."

"And do," she added.

So, not very much later, when the daylight was sifting away in spectacular streaks in the tawny sky over Arlington Cemetery, and Harvey Porter kissed her gently and persuasively on the mouth, Beverly was surprised.

It was she who had asked to see his room—the oriental rug and the marble-topped night table that he had found so splendid in his expense-account accommodations. Having seen and admired, she was on her way back to the lobby sitting room to wait while he changed for dinner. When she found herself standing still, still in the room, with her hand on the brass doorknob. When she found herself reluctant to open the door, realizing with wonderment that she hated to leave him. They were worth analyzing, these feelings, but Beverly did not have a chance, at the time, because Harvey Porter had come across the room to face her and kiss her. Persuasively. On the mouth.

How inappropriate, Beverly thought.

A grandfather with a round belly under his blue sweater. And the beginning of jowls.

How strange.

A mannerly Yankee who had helped her buy presents for her children, who had made her want to be more tolerant of her husband.

How surprising.

There he stood. Unarmed. Only what he was. She looked into his tired, hopeful, ardent blue eyes and saw no disguise in them. And saw that she would not defend herself at this or any other time from this man who drew her heart from its careful hiding place at home.

What the hell, Beverly thought. And kissed him back.

CHAPTER 4 _____

Six weeks before her sudden decision to fly to Washington and look at pictures—activity, activity: it was a trick to ward off a relapse into depression, which, like flu germs, lay in wait for lowered resistance—Beverly Peck Gordon had managed to have a woman-to-woman talk with her increasingly elusive daughter.

For some time Beverly had been watching Allison toss off the bright-eyed kid sisterly mannerisms she had learned from a thousand hours of family television programs and try on the bored drawls and piercing giggles of the insufferable big sisters on the same programs. The adulation of older generations was no longer enough for Allison; she wanted to be popular in school. Her confidental outpourings had been redirected from the home spout to more tortuous outlets in the secret rooms of her contemporaries.

All of which was okay with Beverly, who didn't want to be a clutching mother.

But on the other hand, there was still a place in a daughter's life for motherly guidance and Beverly made her points whenever she got a chance—feeling, though, always feeling for the proper tone of response to the changing modes of her children. On this particular morning in early September—the day, in fact, before Allison's entry into the Heightsville High School—it was a trip to the dentist's office that provided a serviceable stretch of time. Beverly was always glad to chauffeur her kids, now that they were teen-agers, because for one thing it gave her something worthwhile to do and for another it gave her a chance to talk to them.

Allison, who had outgrown the more outward aspects of her brattiness, often faced her mother with a ball in her hand, having caught her between the bases of dealing with the cute kid sister and relating to the sensitive, even sensible young woman. It was true that Allison had been a sitcom kid for so long that Beverly had begun hopefully to believe she might never grow up. And Allison, though twinged by her own growing pains, was complicated enough to understand her mother's ambivalence. Sometimes, when she saw Beverly's sadness spinning through the kitchen in the heat from the dishwasher or rising with the steam from the laundry dryer, she would come softly up from behind and kiss her. Or, as during the long drive to the dentist's office, she would charitably ask a leading question.

Out of the blue of her eyes, she had asked one of her nostalgia questions that were calculated to please her mother and harmlessly beguile the time for Allison.

"So tell me," she said with the perfectly placid face of an Italian fashion model. "Where did you live while you were a career person?"

Beverly fell for it. Besides, it was always a joy to go back.

Beverly Peck would like to have lived (but never to live) in a loft in Soho with rats and cockroaches and perverts in the halls. Or in a cold-water flat on Avenue A that was subject to raids by police in search of drug pushers and runaways. But in truth, as she had to tell it to her daughter, she lived in the Bronx with her parents. "And all of my friends lived home, too, unless they were married right out of college."

"Incredible," Allison said.

"Only an adventuress would move out on her own. And in my family, adventuress was a fancy word for tramp."

"You mean like a whore?"

"Right. My parents were the children of refugees and they inherited a sense of insecurity. They kept their kids close. In a way, it wasn't bad. I got a chance to feel like a rebel without having to do anything really dangerous."

In Allison's imagination, fed so long on a bland suburban diet, the Bronx existed in far space as wild as the Brazilian jungle. Even if she were to become a foreign exchange student or join the Peace Corps, she would never know the excitement that Beverly experienced on her youthful forays into Greenwich Village.

Upstairs at Monte's, downstairs at Eddie's Aurora, around the corner to the New Port Alba, Beverly knew all the cheap restaurants with frayed tablecloths and unheated toilets, none too clean, spotted menus and Chianti that cut your throat, good lasagne, yesterday's bread cold in the basket under a torn napkin, friendly waiters just off the boat, noisy talk, noisy laughter, happy eaters calling from table to table.

That was real life.

Not the Pecks playing cards with their next-door neighbors the Rabinowes. Not reading Wednesday's newspaper ads to see where to shop for the weekend cooking. Not getting all dressed up to go out to a movie.

Real life was the heavy purple smoke afloat like a king's cape in the dark and redolent air of Caffe Reggio, where the foam rose on the *cappuccino* while arty hands pounded out their points on unsteady, marble-topped tables. Real life was Remo, an elegant miniature, a David Rizzio of waiters, who knew Beverly by name and brought the pastry tray with a baroque flourish to the corner table where, in the amber glow of a Tiffany lamp, she and a half dozen comrades hunched in intense discussion of Jean Genet (a jailbird, her mother would have said) and Ezra Pound (that Facist!), the home life of homosexuals (there are some things I'm just as happy not to know, her father would have said, and looked for a newspaper to burrow into), and the stupefying outrage of the Joe McCarthy investigations (listen. where there's smoke, there's usually some fire), and one of them would eventually light a match so they could read the check that Remo had left (what! Sadie Peck would cry out. fifty cents for a little cup of coffee?).

Beverly loved beards and denims in the days when the gray flannel suit was de rigueur. She loved serious music, never dreaming that her life would be marked by a steady advancement down from the last row in the balcony to two seats on the aisle in orchestra center. She loved the wretched apartments of her Village acquaintances because they were so unlike the modern, convenient, efficiently lit ones on the Grand Concourse (the broom closet is out in the hall? you have to walk around the bathtub to get to the toilet? look at that dirty floor!). Beverly, uncritical in her prejudices, preferred books to bric-a-brac, stoneware to china, orange crates to John Widdicomb, and blood and guts to P's and Q's.

However, rents were high in Greenwich Village, so she stayed in the Bronx with her parents.

"No wonder you were a virgin." They were on the way home from the dentist's, Allison smiling with gleaming white teeth. Beverly had let her off, sped to the nearest supermarket, and picked her up a half hour later, plaque-free, polished, and checked for caries. Beverly watched her daughter approach the station wagon, as she often watched her children, from an illusion of distance. She was not altogether comfortable with this new girl with a concavity where her belly used to be. With startling little breasts protruding under her decal T-shirts. With model's slump pushing forward a pelvis which, under patched bluejeans, was bare as a Barbie doll's. With a sad pimple on the chin of a face that used to be rounder and less secretive (in both senses of the word). And a new way of confronting her mother with the kind of firm and logical argument that could not be reasonably defeated: Allison would have been Bat Mitzvah that year but for her clearheaded, irrefutable case against attending Hebrew school. "Besides," she had remarked one night at dinner, after her cause was won, "I'd rather learn French and read Colette in the original."

Now, in the car, homebound after her dental examination, she turned to her mother and said without a trace of childishness:

"No wonder you were a virgin when you got married."

Beverly tried to maintain the appropriate mother-daughter relationship. "Geography," she said in her proper-matron voice, "had nothing to do with it. I was a virgin as a matter of principle."

Allison looked at her with ocean-blue eyes whose depths Beverly was only beginning to acknowledge.

"Besides," Beverly said, "I was scared."

The frequent reversals from Adult/Adult to Parent/Child and even, on occasion, to Child/Child or Child/Parent required an athletic facility that would have staggered parents of other times and places. However, Allison touched her mother's arm and said, "So you never had an affair," and said it with such earnest pity that Beverly had to discard her amusement, her appreciation of the ironies in family evolution, her inherited ideals of refinement and generational propriety, her pride of maternal position, her pleasure in patronizing this child. For Allison was seriously concerned, and what kind of TV-commercial mother, acting from the lack of imagination or courage or conviction, and certainly from the lack of first-class ego-ideals, could go on talking to a sentient, sensible, even sensitive fourteen-year-old person as if she were a caricature?

"No. I never had an affair," Beverly told her daughter. "But it wasn't because I didn't try."

Beverly confessed:

In the old days when I was single and girls and boys were on different sides, a girl would never tell what was really on her mind to anybody but another girl. Boys were for flirting with, flattering, admiring, teasing, manipulating, yearning for, lusting after, sobbing over, and being scared of.

And for marrying.

The fear that I would wake up some morning and find my face wrinkled and no man wanting to marry me was never completely out of my mind.

I know there were numbers of my female contemporaries who went to bed with men to whom they were not married. But not my friends. Or if they did, they were smart enough not to tell me.

But I knew it was being done. I had not gone to college blindfolded. I knew that Alice Weiss did it with Frank Goldsmith but they were engaged. And Shirley LaPonte had done it with Bob Meyer but that was because they'd gotten carried away during a fraternity weekend. Margaret Dwarkin did it with Lenny Pincus because she needed to prove she was a woman and then she did it with Paul Progoff and Victor Klansky just to make sure. Jill Tanenbaum had a guilty conscience from doing it and she took nightly showers that were so hot they turned her body into an all-over blush. Kathy Jordan did it with anyone who asked her because she came from a broken home and felt insecure. And Lydia Morgenstern kept a pocket diary with a numerical listing of everyone she did it with. I would have sworn Lydia was on the road to harlotry but she got married to Number 17, 18, 19, and all the way up after 22 and they have three kids and live in New Milford, New Jersey, where he is on the Borough Council and she is the president of the League of Women Voters.

I blamed my virginity on my parents. Whenever I found myself in the dark with someone I liked being in the dark with,

I started to think about how upset my parents would be if they found out. I started to think *what if he loses respect for me?* I started to be afraid he wouldn't call in the morning. I started to feel pregnant and I could—in the scared Jewish corner of my mind, a corner like Times Square—hear my parents telling me they told me so.

"What did they tell you?" Allison was skeptical.

"Listen," Beverly said. "If you had been brought up by your Grandmother Sadie, you'd be frigid, too. She used to tell me that men are like dogs, always sniffing around."

"Even Grandpa?"

It was a question Beverly had never thought to ask.

"The point is, " she told her daughter, "that I was always a little nervous about sex."

"I don't know why you just didn't shack up with one of your boyfriends."

"In those days, Allison, a smart girl didn't go to bed with marriage material. She'd be risking her best chances."

However, Beverly reassured her daughter, who was unmistakably appalled at this mercantile viewpoint, she herself did not want to chance being a lifelong virgin. She had set a whimsical limit at age twenty-two: "And to make sure I beat the deadline, I started to take singing lessons."

"You used to want to be a singer?"

"Of course not."

It was through her association with the tenor Gregorio that Beverly met the Maestro. All of Gregorio's friends—students, like him, who were certain that with time, practice, and good breaks they would become stars of the Metropolitan

Opera—were instantaneous friends of Beverly's; Adele, a so-
prano with a heaving bosom and trembling chin; Patrick, by
his own description a three-balled baritone, whose powerful
voice rose from deep between his football shoulders. Beverly
thirty-nine remembered Beverly twenty sitting cross-legged on
spring grass singing duets with Patrick. Red-headed Richard, a
tenor like Gregorio, worked at the Fiftieth Street Nedick's and
gave free orange drinks to his friends when the manager wasn't
looking. Lillian, an older, married woman, a fierce intellectual, with a sad limp, ran a continuous open house for musi-
cians, where, as in Beverly's favorite opera *La Bohème*, the
sounds of music were continually cut into by passionate argument and bravura laughter. Gregorio the tenor was the
warmest, gayest, most romantic one of all: (Beverly thirty-nine
still knew him slightly as the cantor of a Reform temple not
very far from Heightsville). He was short, like all tenors, with
broad cheeks and a square jaw. He claimed to have, like all
tenors, no head for business, so he made Beverly his manager.

Beverly's current job availed her of a desk and unlimited
telephone privileges, so it was dashingly easy for her to be a
singer's manager. She even managed once to find a job for her
client by telephoning a radio station and talking to a secretary
and meeting a program producer and arranging an audition
which led to an engagement on a local radio show called the
Italian Musical Hour though it was only a half-hour show.
Beverly's manager's commission—mutually agreed upon as
ten percent of Gregorio's pay—amounted to five dollars and
two cans of imported Italian tomato sauce. However, the most
fateful tangent of her managerial career was her meeting with
Gregorio's voice coach, Dr. Branko Paulik, known as the
Maestro.

Dr. Paulik was a dream man, Beverly saw at once. The body of an athlete; the head of an artist. A great weight of worldliness. He had iron-gray hair and irony in his smile . . .

Allison interrupted her mother at this point: "Gray hair?"
"Right . . . He was an older man. Maybe forty."
"Like Daddy," Allison pointed out.

Dr. Paulik lived and taught on West Seventy-second Street, a place of particular enchantment because it was full of singing studios and beautiful in fair weather when windows were open and strong arches of music—scales, arpeggios, song passages—soared from one side of the street to the other over the sounds of traffic and the scents from the Viennese bakery and the Jewish delicatessen and the Turkish coffee shop, all of which reminded Beverly with delicious poignancy of a Europe she had never seen.

Dr. Paulik himself was European, a former Bulgarian basso who had sung Don Giovanni, Mephistopheles. When Gregorio introduced Beverly, the Maestro took her extended hand, turned it over, and kissed it.

His studio-apartment appealed to Beverly twenty because it was unfashionable and bookish. She loved the low-slung couch with worn flowered upholstery, the faded oriental rug, the monstrous old lamp with a green fringe around a pagoda-shaped shade. She was susceptible to the old molding and the tall framed windows that let in the smoked rose of summer sunsets when she and Gregorio stayed late after his lessons, and the rising tiers of books, the heads of great composers reverently displayed, and, of course, the grand piano upon which the Maestro played while Gregorio sang and Beverly watched from one of the dumpy armchairs, feeling herself to be a genuine woman of the world.

Dr. Paulik and Gregorio played a musical version of follow-the-leader, a chord by the Maestro setting off a flight of notes by Gregorio that rose and returned for a landing just in time to catch the key of the next chord. After some twenty minutes of warming up—the voice open, stretched, flexible, flowing—the real singing began with the Maestro's big hands gently stroking the keys as he bent under the musical line and instructed his pupil, coaxed him, exhorted him, soothed him: "More slowly, my son, and with more expression." So tenderly urged and supported, Gregorio climbed to heights of beautiful song and the twenty-year-old Beverly was stirred by a lesson that was in itself a work of art.

In the down elevator, Gregorio was jubilant: "The Maestro likes you!"

Moving tentatively through her first cosmopolitan summer, Beverly had let her hair grow long and wore it wantonly loose with strings of beads around her neck and, as soon as she could collect enough money for them, leather sandals hand-made at a shop on West Fourth Street where an artisan traced the outline of her foot in black crayon on brown paper. Dr. Paulik, like many another teacher of a certain age, was probably invigorated by the proximity and trust of his youthful pupils and moved by the moist-eyed adulation of the young women to think of playing a romantic part in their lives. Beverly at twenty, fresh, poignantly fleshy, heartbreakingly alive, was hard to overlook—and her susceptibility was clear. On her part, she knew that the Maestro had simply opened the door, moved in, and taken over (NO VACANCY) her dream life. Tantalizing pieces of Dr. Paulik shot like meteoric images through the tightly woven texture of her ordinary, organized thoughts. His hands on the keyboard. A stretch of neck and chest at his open collar. The iron forearm with dark veins pulsing under a rolled-up sleeve. A severe patch of face from nostril to cheek. Nothing below the waist, of course. Beverly twenty fantasized like the Saturday movies she had grown up on: kiss and blackout. Yet rippling through the freeze of her insoluble combinations of appetite and inhibition, sophisticated notions and primitive fears, contemporary daring and the domesticating admonitions of her parents and collective generations of her lost ancestors came a fierce bubble of recognition that Dr. Paulik was precisely the right man to break the curse of her virginity, to press the awakening kiss on her torpid libido; in short: to make a woman of her before it was too late.

By that time Beverly knew him well enough to know he would be the perfect lover. She had sat between him and Gregorio at his pupils' performances, enveloped with him in mutual music appreciation. She had been in circles—at Lillian's parties, in coffeehouses—at the center of which a towering Maestro made carefully weighed, wistfully ironic pronouncements on music and politics and history and philosophy, lightening his profundity with little jokes that the members of his group savored and repeated among themselves for a week after. Most impressive of all, she had watched many times as he worked with Gregorio: "Do not force," Dr. Paulik told his pupil. "Let the voice flow freely. In time strength will come." Beverly took long breaths and waited until the day that the Maestro suggested that she come to him for singing lessons: singing is good for the soul and the speaking voice.

"I can't believe you, Mother. You were twenty?"

"Twenty-one by that time. No one could say I was hasty."

"Let the voice flow over the breath," the Maestro said. He was wearing a blood-red velours shirt unzipped almost to the waist. His hair curled away from its combing in perverse little forks like puffs of smoke. He leaned far back on the piano stool, stretching away from the sound of the keys so that he could hear the sound of Beverly, humming through pressed lips. His eyes were half closed, the better to hear her. It made her nervous but she followed his instructions: hummed the open chords, sang them in syllables—*may. mah, may, mah, may, mah, may*—to relax her throat, which was very tight. The exercise worked, and from traveling up and down the keys, her voice began to loosen and soon she was reaching high notes with astounding comfort. "Beverly is singing now," Dr. Paulik said with large satisfaction.

Then he told her it was time to practice with the diaphragm.

Beverly understood his meaning, but all the same—teetering as she was on the elastic rim of a plunge into sexuality—it gave her a start.

She tried to fill her abdomen with breath.

The Maestro was patient. "Sometimes it is easier lying down," he suggested.

"You want me to lie down?"

"It is sometimes easier."

Beverly got down on the couch as if she were waiting for a doctor to examine a lump. She would have jumped up again but there was no way to jump up without revealing her hysteria. So she stretched out with her sandals on and her skirt pulled over her knees and hated herself for the crossed circuits that made her distrust Dr. Paulik at the very same time she wanted him with all her heart—or at least a good deal of it—to seduce her. She couldn't look at his face and when she lowered her eyes she saw with an internal gasp of aggravated apprehension that he was wearing European trousers with a button fly.

And a bulge.

So when she put her hand on her diaphragm to feel the breath come in and he put his hand on top of hers and she stared straight ahead at the terrible lamp with the pagoda shade, what she saw was that the green tassels hanging from the fringe around the edge of the lampshade had become a hundred index fingers all shaking a solemn warning at her, and past them the tall windows stood like two disapproving sentries behind dotted swiss curtains.

Dr. Paulik was on one knee, coaxing her to breathe in, breathe out. "Feel as the diaphragm expands," he said, moving his hand over her hand while the statuettes of Verdi and Puccini discreetly turned their backs. The Maestro was leaning close. "Deep," he said. "Breathe deep." He was stroking her arm. "Only relax as if you are floating on a boat of clouds . . ."

It was lovely to float, breathing in, breathing out, softly to float on the waves of the flow'ry sofa, floating in the deepening mauve-gold light of the beautiful floating room where beautiful music flowed forever floating . . .

Beverly inhaled luxuriously, her limp hand rising high with the waves, the Maestro's hand rising over hers. The Maestro was breathing more deeply, too. Together floating, warming, breathing, expanding. "That is right, my love," he said and kissed her on the temple.

Beverly thought, with relief and release, that she was finally doing it. The Maestro's arms slipped around her and his lips separated as he bent toward her lips. She took her last virginal breath and gazed—yielding—up at the Maestro and noticed for the first time since she had met him that there was a space between his upper front teeth.

A gap. Between his teeth.

She sat up like a splash of ice water, "I think I've got it all right now. Don't you think I have it right?"

Dr. Paulik was a graceful man though his patience was sorely stretched. He tried for a little while longer, but his moment had passed. His hopes, her dreams marched in double file out of the studio to the sound of drumming:

gap teeth gap teeth gap teeth

"And so," said Beverly thirty-nine, who in less than six weeks would be lost in the arms and the intensity of a man she did not yet know, "I decided to save myself for my husband." Allison already knew the legend of the meeting of Beverly Peck and Peter Gordon on an August weekend when the parents of the former were visiting cousins who lived next door to the aunt and uncle of the latter in a Catskill Mountain cottage colony. Peter was, like Beverly, a college graduate. He was two years older than she, had finished his army service, and was ready to start real life. Like Beverly, he couldn't sing. When his parents met her parents, it was love at first sight. The marriage, all of them standing under a flower-strewn canopy, took place the following June, just before Beverly's twenty-second birthday.

"And you lived happily ever after," Allison reminded her mother.

"That's right," Beverly said.

By that time they were parked in their driveway, but Allison was not in her usual hurry to leave the car. "You know what?" she said from a little Japanese shell in her head that had begun to open and issue bouquets of flamboyantly floating ideas. "I don't intend to be as puritanical as you when I grow up."

"Scared," Beverly corrected her.

CHAPTER 5 _____

Beverly Peck Gordon wandered through the subterranean passages of her thirteen-years-late postpartum depression mole-blind and frozen into torpor but still somehow keeping in touch with her family, who were functioning as usual on ground level and only peripherally aware that their wife, mother, daughter, in-law Beverly was not quite up to her customary standards in breadth of smile, luminosity of eye, readiness to say Yes, to put on coffee, to throw a coat over her nightshirt and pick up whoever was out late and needed a ride home, to turn a peg and tune herself in to the mood required by the occasion and the mode of response sought by the indi-

vidual. Her children did not see her, sad-faced at the supermarket, as she lingered in stupefaction gazing at comparative
ketchup bottles or stood wilting on the endless checkout line,
too hopeless even to try to read the captions under the photo-
graphs on the covers of the scandal sheets. Her husband did
not notice how, on the mornings when she drove him to the
bus station, something behind her eyes flew up like a
frightened flock of birds when he asked his friendly, mechanical question: "What are your plans for today?"

But during those early weeks, as her eyes became accustomed to the dark and she was gradually able to move slowly
through the tunnels of her grief, she began to observe a pro-
gression of moving tableaus, grotesque pantomimes with the
phantom figures and ragged costumes and spindly props of
street theater, fearful in the obliquity of their gaudy lighting
and enacted on stages that were no more than jagged excavations in the ancient, petrified walls along her primitive path.

Peter Gordon is going on another business trip. Middle of
winter. Acapulco or Nassau. No wives, but Beverly can come
if she wants to. Beverly can't: what if it snows and the kids need
a ride to school? What if? Beverly, truly happy that Peter will
get the benefit of some vitamin D sunshine plus a much
needed rest, kisses him goodby. Smiles. Waves. Feels the beginning twinge of psychosomatic vaginitis.

Sandy is having a party. He has fixed up the family room
single-handed. Bought Cheese Doodles and cans of soda.
Moved in his stereo, his records. Set down floor cushions,
beanbag chairs. Turned out the lights. Twenty or thirty
thirteen-year-olds. Beverly offered to make hot dogs, a cake.

Sandy protested: "It's not like birthday parties. Parents stay away. Upstairs if not out." But Beverly can't resist. The kids are so cute. Maybe, toward midnight, they'd like a tray of cookies and some chocolate milk. Beverly knocks but cannot be heard over the rock. Opens the door a crack and sweet smoke squeezes out. The sequin lights of cigarette tips. Children in heaps. Girls and boys. No sound but the rock and deep inhalations. Sandy's voice, distant, from a shadow: "Nobody wants cookies." Beverly, foolish intruder, backs out with her platter, no place to put it.

Marjorie Sparrow, fellow library mother, stops over one afternoon with a petition. Beverly, civic-minded citizen, knows the story: Heightsville needs a new junior high school. Which of the two available locations to build on? The north side would mean a busy intersection for the schoolkids to cross and furthermore a row of four small houses would have to be condemned to make room for a playing field. The east side property is safer .and sounder since no families would be displaced and it is also more centrally located. Marjorie Sparrow agrees with Beverly that the east side, for both humane and practical reasons, is the better location.

In theory.

However, east side householders have formed a Neighborhood Group to promote the north side location and keep their streets clear of cars and children. While Marjorie Sparrow agrees that the east side Neighborhood Group is acting primarily from self-concern, there is another aspect to be considered. (No, she really can't stay long enough for coffee but it is kind of Beverly to ask.) Has Beverly considered how close the east side site is to the town line between Heightsville and Burntwood? Did she know about the problems at Burntwood High School? (Marjorie Sparrow is not prejudiced and understands the socio-economic roots of the problems. Still, academic standards have dropped at Burntwood and many families have been forced to put their children in private school.) If Heightsville were to build a new school so close to Burntwood, Marjorie Sparrow suggests, it just might occur to troublemakers that a ninety-five percent white school and a sixty percent black school were situated within two miles of one another and they might want to shake things up. (Marjorie Sparrow has a face like a birthday present, even with anxiety shining through her eyes.) She speaks to Beverly's concern for her children, for their education as well as their physical well-being. She speaks to Beverly's concern for the quality of the community that has been so hospitable to both their families. Beverly and Marjorie Sparrow are united—are they not?—in their mutual dedication to the preservation of the character of their schools.

Beverly signs the petition on behalf of the north side location, thereby adding one more notch to a belt that had not yet begun to choke her.

Sandy has been to the fair. It is late summer and he is newly eleven years old, stocky, solid, with the Gordons' black curls and his own sober, amber eyes now fired with fear as his father bears down on him. "Ten dollars at an amusement park? Do you think I'm made of money?"

Peter's anger is growing out of him—his mouth, his ears, his eyes—like a huge, revved-up jungle plant filling Sandy's room, choking off the double-decker bed and the orderly desk, blocking the pennants on the wall and the Erector models on the shelves of the bookcase. Sandy knows this anger. "It was my own money," he says. He is trying not to cringe. "Billy Bradley had a lot, too. Eddie Ford spent sixteen dollars."

Peter's face is like a jungle rock. "I don't care about the other kids. Maybe their fathers don't work as hard as I do."

"But it was my birthday money. Mommy said I could spend it as I like."

"Oh, yes. Big sport. My son, the spender. Walks around like a big gun. Shows off for his fancy friends." A snarling eruption lifts the room from its foundation. "What do you think this is? What do you contribute to this house? When did you lift a hand?" Beverly watches helplessly as Sandy, with humiliating tears, says he is sorry and Peter's unfathomable, implacable anger continues to strangle everything in the room, making it almost impossible to breathe. "I'm going to strap you," Peter says and is undoing his belt as Beverly flies at him and he shoves her murderously aside. "Oh, please. Please." Sandy is doubled over his disgrace with his nose running and loud sounds of fear and shame and despair coming out of his mouth. Beverly runs to protect his body.

Peter reached the height of pride and joy at his son's Bar Mitzvah. He had always been a hard worker, ever since his father Max had got him up at six o'clock in the morning to help unload the dry goods delivery truck. Peter knew how to work hard and hard work made him feel good. As he stood among his guests, watching them eat, drink, dance, enjoy themselves, he could see and they could see that his labor had borne fruit. For Sandy was the ego extension, the reason and reward for Peter's hard work. He hoped the boy would appreciate it.

Beverly had a dream: They are all in the front seat of a Cadillac coupe de ville. Daddy is driving, Allison between him and the door, Sandy between Daddy and Mommy. Mommy is looking out the window, gazing grazingly, happy as usual to be chauffeured.

It is a hot day; a butter sun melts on them.

They are driving in the city; it is hot and crowded.

Mommy turns now to graze on her family but sees with growing embarrassment that they are crowded, pushed torturously close together, suffering in the damp heat, sweating against the synthetic leather seat back, hot, uncomfortable, breathing with difficulty while she has plenty of room. She is sitting in a pleasant enclosure of cool air. They are pinched together at the other end of the sliding seat. She is affected with a spread of horror. "Oh, dear!" she cries, now damp herself with a sweat of shame. "I'm crowding you!" She pushes herself into her own corner. "I don't need all this space!" she cries. "There's room for us all!

"I'm so sorry. Why didn't someone tell me?"

"A letdown is natural," Peter told Beverly. "You did a great job. It was your production. You handled all the details. And it was beautiful."

Peter had no regrets. The Bar Mitzvah was worth everything. An occasion to remember. But a week or two after it was over, his home life started to go sour. Beverly, formerly cheerful, a little bit featherheaded sometimes, but always agreeable, started to feel glum.

Peter understood. She was used to a lot of attention and he had been unusually busy lately. So he took her to a show. They had dinner out. But she was glum. Nothing could cheer her up.

Then she became afraid. She hated to see Peter leave in the morning. She said she had the horrors. Maybe she was anemic; maybe she had mononucleosis. He took her to the doctor. She was fine. But she walked around scared. She did her work. She kept up the house. But she lost her laughter. She saw everything dark and the darkness took over the house. The kids were uneasy with eyes full of questions that Peter couldn't answer.

It was summertime, so he took two weeks off and he took them all on a vacation to a big resort in New Hampshire, where the kids could go swimming and horseback riding and Beverly didn't have to cook. She seemed to feel better there. But Peter was uneasy, for he knew that women approaching forty sometimes get into serious emotional problems and that would be all he needed, a sick wife. So when they got back from their vacation, he was more attentive than ever. He hurried home at night and he called during the day and he did everything, everything he could—as he had always done anyway, come to think of it—to make her happy. Gradually, she felt better. But she came out of it with a lot of strange ideas. She wanted Peter to define his goals.

Beverly left a note pinned to the top T-shirt in Peter's pile of clean underwear:

If I knew what you wanted, I could try to help you get it. Or I could decide that I wanted something different and argue about it. At present, I'm hanging on to the back of a bus and I don't know where it's going.

Peter's first reply (undelivered):

I don't want any help from you. Just go your own way and leave me alone. Be happy. Be good. And don't bother my head.

Peter's second reply (undelivered):

*I want what I have. My wife's love and devotion. My chil-
dren's respect. Peace and quiet in my house. Satisfaction from
my business. A little less fighting from the kids. Chicken more
often. Maybe livelier bedroom scenes, a little more movement,
a little more enthusiasm. What does any man want? I want
what my father had. I am content. I love you.*

Peter's third reply (delivered orally late in the night, after
he had wearily pulled off the very T-shirt the note had been
pinned to):

"I do not," Peter told Beverly, who had been reading in
bed for an hour, "have the luxury of asking metaphysical questions about where I'm going. I go to the office and knock my
balls together so I can finish up and come home and pay the
bills. You want to know where the bus is heading? It's running
to keep up with the bill collector. That's all it can do."

As the Bar Mitzvah depression lifted, Beverly thought
things would be better.

"I mean it, Peter. I'm willing to get a job."

"Come down to earth. I know you. It would cost more for
you to work than if you stayed home. You'll buy clothes.
You'll take taxis. You'll be wanting to eat out all the time. I
know you. You wouldn't make enough to cover expenses."

"That isn't true. If I went to work to help you save money,
I certainly wouldn't spend it all."

"Face the facts, Bev. You're not going to give up your
luncheons. Your tennis. Your yoga class. And your two-hour
telephone conversations with your girl friends. Besides, who's
going to keep up this big house of yours?"

"We could get a smaller house. We don't need such a big
place. You don't have to feel saddled."

"Sure. Sure. You could live in a small house. Where

would you entertain all your friends? Where would you put
your fancy furniture? I know you. You wouldn't be happy in a
smaller house."

"Then let me get a job."

"What are you talking about? What can you do?"

It was dangerous to push him. He retracted, pulling into
himself, making his surface as smooth and hard as rock. She
was afraid to push too hard. She knew what happened when
she went past the line of discretion.

"What do I ever do for myself? What do you want from
me? Do you want my blood?"

Yes. Of course. It was no less than his blood that she
wanted.

There was no possible reply. It was dangerous to jump off
the back of a bus in the middle of traffic.

"Everything I do is for you and the kids." This was his
theme. He used to play the tune when Beverly asked about
carpeting, summer camp, a new dress, a dinner party. He sang
his song and she danced her dance and it ended, sooner or
later, with his consent and her gratitude. But after the Bar
Mitzvah depression, the theme had begun to develop with
thunderous undertones. With every outward move that Beverly made, the rock grew harder and the rage burst more
lethally from its hot center.

"What do you want from me?"

They were talking about change and it was no longer a
musical situation.

By the time Beverly Peck Gordon flew to Washington and

met what later proved to be the love of her life in the totally unpredictable form of a gray and portly Yankee lawyer, she had often returned to review these blistering scenes in the glaring light of a desperate present and she had loosened and re-tied the laces of her personality as hopeful insurance that the same abrasions would not recur to cripple her again. Three years after the Bar Mitzvah depression, Beverly had become a new woman. She was a new woman who, in her walking shoes and casual clothes, had no handbag, gloves, or girdle to encumber her, no pockets or folds in which to fit a dehydrated relic of the old woman or even of the twenty-year-old girl she used to be, though there remained in and about her (as Harvey Porter recognized in the heat and depth of his love) the light of all the other Beverlys from ever and beyond.

CHAPTER 6

Something crashingly tender and undemanding in the embrace of Harvey Porter made Beverly step in to return his kiss, slipping her arms around his soft blue sweater under his arms around her corduroy coat because he was only a few inches taller than she. Feeling the comfort of his roundness, the sincerity of his round bones as he held her against him, she was suddenly overcome by a primeval tenderness of her own, which made her forget to step back again and walk out of the room.

Instead, she looked into Harvey Porter's warm, cloudless eyes and saw that she could possibly save him from premature burial in the autumn leaves and winter snows that were piling deeper and deeper around him in Waddingford, Connecticut. Saving him was selfishly important, for she saw also in the sky of his eyes a Beverly who could fly high and free. And at the same moment she saw that in her heart there was a small, desert place—fenced off from family, neighbors, sense of duty—where an unnamed and unrecognized longing was growing in dry sand so that when Harvey Porter had helped her off with her rumpled coat and had carefully hung it in the closet beside his neatly pressed one, she could hardly wait for him to turn around and take her into his arms again.

Harvey Porter took her so gently into his arms that she almost fell backwards. "I'm not used to this," she said. "I get grabbed a lot. I get bear hugs."

"I don't want to hurt you."

He smiled at her.

She noticed a space between his left cuspid and left side incisor and saw again that his teeth were stained from to-bacco.

It didn't matter.

He kissed her again and she wondered why she had always been afraid of gentleness. He kissed her again and she rejoiced that she had not put on one of her acts for this man. She had come to him without makeup and without politesse. Whatever she was—unvarnished, ungarnished—was what he wanted and he touched her as if she were precious.

Beverly went limp and fell in love, signed herself over. Harvey Porter's kisses reached to the little parched plant of her longing, which suddenly and magically grew long, lustrous leaves to embrace him. Beverly kissed the dejected corner of his mouth, his cheek, his double chin, the crow's-foot patch beside his eye, the mouth again and licked his lips, his tongue, and kissed him, kissing away years of marital lovemaking that had occupied, interested, and often satisfied her but had never, in all its physical and emotional variations, nourished that last, deep corner of her heart. Safe in a strong man's arms, she sighed a sigh which grew to be as big as a bubble and bigger until it was as big and beautiful as a glass moon, which encompassed her as she fell into it and did not even try to pick herself up again.

"Shall we undress?"

Beverly was confused. So happily bundled in the bubble with Harvey Porter, what more could there be? The suggestion of nudity startled her. Naked, with a stranger? Thank God for her years of Tuesday morning yoga classes, where she had learned to look at herself, a no-bull mirror image in leotard and tights, and respect the shape and strength of her body. Beverly could balance on one leg and tip forward till the free leg was as high and straight behind her as a sparrow's tail. She could lie on her back with both legs over her head and touch her knees to the floor behind her. Sitting with spread legs, she could hold her feet and almost reach the floor with her forehead. Kneeling, she could flatten out backwards and pick herself up again. She knew she was firm and properly aligned, in better shape for her age than anybody had a right to expect. And in the flash of no time, as she stared into the shock of Harvey Porter's suggestion, she was suddenly overjoyed to be giving him this bonus. At the same time, being totally inexperienced at unmarried sex, she was alarmed.

"Are we going to just neck or go all the way?"

"We'll leave it to artistic necessity."

"I quit the pill. I've been reading about hormones causing

blood clots and cancer. And of course I didn't think to bring my diaphragm."

Harvey Porter said he had had a vasectomy some years earlier.

Beverly burrowed blissfully into the hills and hollows of his not statuesque but wondrously male physique.

"Yeah?" she whispered because she couldn't talk. "Let me see your papers."

He was startled. "Papers?"

But Beverly was already zipping off her skirt, kicking off her shoes, rolling down pantyhose, tossing aside a T-shirt, and flying in her bra and pants to stand in front of him, terrified and exultant, as still as she could manage to stand, perfectly serious now, in the dim light from the Stiffel lamp, to have him venture along her almost unbearably waiting surfaces, her breasts rising and nipples pursing like lips reaching to a kiss. Every edge of fabric, hairline, body contour became an occasion for excruciating suspense and breakthrough as she stood breathless and undefended against the slow and knowing explorations of his soft, small, ineffably gentle hands. Harvey Porter could not laugh or shake his head but only lose himself in the wonder of this implausible woman who was already beginning to unbutton his shirt as he was trying to elbow out of his soft blue sweater.

In the past he had permitted himself an occasional, surreptitious hour with a book of erotic art or literature, which aroused him and which he afterward enjoyed thinking about. But Beverly Gordon was like nothing he had ever dreamed of during the quiet evenings by the fire in his old frame house in Waddingford. He undid the hooks of her bra. He knelt to slip off her bikini pants, Outside on M Street, time's wingless chariots clattered by. But he and Beverly did not hear them. His clothes were in a neat, square pile on the dresser; hers were strewn over floor, armchair, lampshade.

"What do you call your pretty place?"

He was kissing her there.

"Cunt," Beverly said.

He loved it. He loved her. And she so much loved his loving that she actually shut up, turned off, faded out, and didn't utter a sound except for, once in a long while, the tiniest chirp of incredulity or the stillest sigh of rapture.

"I can scarcely believe that we are here," Harvey said. And once he said, "I love you," as if he really didn't want to, and Beverly, not wanting it either, felt for his mouth and touched it shut. Love had always been expensive. It was not a gift she could accept without suspicion, fear, and a wary assessment of contingencies. So she simply clung to her bed partner and reveled in the beautiful and inventive ways in which he stated and developed and modulated the theme of his love with a growing excitement and urgency not at all out of line with the shape of his lovemaking but instead building to climax after climax so that coupling with Harvey Porter became an aesthetic as well as an erotic experience that left Beverly calm as a cloud and for once in her life, free, at least temporarily, from fighting the Gentiles, the Jews, the nicely-nicelies, the Women's Liberation Movement, the powers that were and had been, for the right to be—at least some of the time—nothing to, for, by, because of, in spite of, for the sake of anybody else but Beverly.

"It is a miracle," Harvey Porter said.

And then his penchant for pain showed up. "How will I ever be able to say goodby to you?"

"Screw goodby," Beverly said. "We're just saying hello."
"Goodby is for tomorrow," she said.

Her undecorated white bra dangled from the shade of the
bed-table lamp on which Harvey Porter, in a moment of abandon, had abandoned it.

Later, after the lights were off and on and off again, after
the fitted bedspread and the fine percale top sheet and all the
real down pillows were heaped and strewn about the room and
after the brass bedposts had spun north, south, east, and west,
Beverly knew that Harvey Porter had a small, white behind
and a roll of flab around his middle and that, while not struc-
turally the man of any dream that had entertained her, he was
yet the most beautiful of all possible lovers, and Harvey Porter
knew that Beverly, having opened herself to him without restraint or reservation, had helped him to reach a previously
unidentified core of his being where an invincible youth rose
and stretched himself in the sunlight. And later, when they
had thought about calling room service for dinner and decided
that they would rather wait until much later and Beverly had
noticed that Harvey was the kind of man who puts the toilet
seat down when he is finished and Harvey had noticed that
Beverly was the kind of woman who does not look away when
a man walks naked across the room and after Beverly had
three kinds of orgasms which she knew she would not describe
for her feminist friend Mollie Parish's Orgasm Survey that was
to be published in an upcoming issue of *Continental*
magazine, Harvey—wrapped like a Turk in a tent-size Madison hotel bath towel—sat on the edge of the bed and looked at
Beverly stretched naked like Olympia and said again, "It will
be torture to leave you" and Beverly said, "Shut up" and rolled

over and knocked him flat and kissed his lips and his temples and the tired place under his eyes and his pale pointed nipples and his flaccid belly and cried out at last with astonishment:

"You aren't circumcised!"

"I'm not Jewish, you know."

"I know." And she studied and touched the amazing hood of his foreskin and then kissed him again on his straight Wasp mouth that pulled on every kiss as if Harvey Porter were trying to suck her into him and keep her there. He took her face in his hands and held her still while he said again, "I love you," and this time she had to drop her eyes to avoid meeting the emotion in his.

Love! She pulverized the word and flung the love dust up against the ceiling and out the windows to sprinkle down on the roofs of midnight taxicabs on M street. She curled herself around Harvey and slipped her hand under his towel. "You are a beautiful fucker," she said and his neck turned red as a radish ("Guess what's a Jewish strawberry?" she asked him) and she could not resist nuzzling him—Yankee neck, Yankee shoulders, Yankee chest—until he caught her again in his arms.

"You don't talk like a suburban housewife," the beautiful fucker, needing a rest, observed. "I would say that you have a salty vocabulary. While the intonation suggests the New York City area, the style of speech might argue that you had spent some time in the U.S. Navy disguised as a seaman."

"Actually, I learned it in graduate school. Where I go to school, it would be an unpardonable *gaffe* to use a euphemism."

The brass bed smelled of sweat and satisfied sex and Beverly could see that it was time for a break though she hated to break the bubble. "I am a bit weary," she said and was amazed at herself for showing such consideration of Harvey's feelings. While he slipped on some clothes to wait for room service with bourbon and ice and she hid under the covers because she was in no mood for clothes or drinking, she told him a thing or two about State U. and how it had contributed to her fall from gentility.

"Did you ever have a really good fuck?"

The question was aimed at Ms. Gordon by her fellow student Mr. Hendersen, who stared at her with double-barreled, bloodshot hostility from across the table at their seminar in Contemporary Poetry.

Beverly was not vexed. Free language was not alien to a woman who had drummed into her children when they were young: *there are no dirty words, only dirty minds (but don't use the dirty words in front of your grandparents)*. At State U., where it would be anathema to "throw up" or "go to the bathroom," she had quickly learned to call a black man a spade and rid herself of any bad habits she had picked up in the suburbs.

"I mean," Hendersen continued with clear and present malice, " a really terrific, stars and stripes, bombs bursting in air kind of fuck."

The whole class was waiting.

Beverly had already accepted as an occupational hazard of the middle-aged college returnee the possibility that one member of any class, if not the teacher himself, would take a look at her and see an index of all the crimes, remembered and imagined, that his mother had perpetrated upon him from the moment of his traumatic eviction from the womb. From her first doubtful day at college, a day of standing on one long line after another for faculty advice, for registration, for course permission, for payment of tuition, for a student identification card on which there would be pasted an instamatic, smearily colored photograph of a woman looking as expended and forlorn as her ancestors might have felt after their day on Ellis Island, Beverly had recognized that she was different from her fellow students: older. And she saw that most of the students were friendly, sympathetic, respectful, or, at least, indifferent. But by the end of that long, confusing, wearying, and stimulating day, she had also seen that there would always be a few young people who would automatically dislike her not because she was Jewish (as in Heightsville) or American (as in Paris) or a woman (as in business dealings) or a liberal (as in party conversation), but because she was obviously over thirty-five and managing to keep herself together. All, for example, that Lars Hendersen had to see was a woman of a certain age— neat, polite, apparently regular in living habits—for him to be run straight up the peeling classroom wall by a horde of sado-masochistic furies. Therefore, when Hendersen, with his red eyes, messianic haircut, and impoverished overalls stuffed into sixty-five-dollar tooled leather boots, tried to make a poetic point by challenging her middle-class, middle-age prudery, Beverly was not too shaken to reply with equanimity:

"More than one, thank God."

It wasn't such a great comeback, she realized.

But it was acceptable.

There were twelve students in the Contemporary Poetry seminar though, Beverly had noticed with interest, a different twelve at each semi-weekly session. Most of the regulars were recent liberal arts graduates who were working toward a master's degree so that they could get jobs as English teachers or get into doctoral programs so that they could get better jobs as English teachers. The truants, she suspected, were working (or not working) for a master's degree primarily because they didn't want to get jobs. Though they met in an ancient building, in an overheated room with flaking ceiling and cracked windows, a classroom—Beverly ruefully reflected—that could justifiably incite a demonstration at State Prison, all the students, regular and absentee, seemed oblivious to the discomforts and even unaware that their illustrious professor, Elliot Leighton himself, had turned out to be only a helium-filled replica of a literary hero. Having shown up at the first session in a pleated skirt and sweater (loafers, too!), she had felt like a visitor from a nostalgic musical revue, something like Big Band Beverly Co-ed, among the saris, dashikis, and army surplus clothing of her classmates. Downcast she felt, sliding back into her coalpit, so recently and painfully escaped, and worse she felt when her only near contemporary, the professor himself, the famous poet, made his own late entrance (behind a disarray of books and lecture notes) in filthy bluejeans and a bunchy purple polo shirt.

After eight weeks, though, the students no longer looked all the same to her. Beverly knew that the sari was a welfare mother named Paula, who ran her life with the help of Tarot cards and cooked dinner every night for her children and their baby-sitter and her boyfriend's children and theirs; that the knapsack was a part-time youth worker named Terri, who also wrote polemic poetry for the underground newspaper *Up Yours*; that the dashiki with the foot-high afro was a New Leftist named Ivory Johnson, who posed nude for art classes so that she could save enough money to move out of her parents' apartment in the Bronx not far from the Grand Concourse building in which Beverly had grown up; and that everybody in the class except Beverly had at least done pot and acid and mescaline or, if they hadn't, said they had anyway, and Beverly knew that she and these people really got along.

So when she told Lars Hendersen that she had, thank God, more than a single good fuck to remember, all the others had let out their held breath and sent their vibrations of approval and support around the table to her, a woman they saw not as a threatening mother but as an engaged fellow student who gratefully acknowledged the fact that the receiving set in her head was still in working order over sixteen years after the automatic turnoff on the day of her last college examination. They saw she was amazed at how much life there was still left in the world. And they saw in her eyes reflections of themselves as lovable for their contributions to the exuberance, innocence, truculence, sharpness, bluntness, untrammeledness, immoderation, laziness, craziness, vulnerability, and utter lostness that abounded in the Contemporary Poetry seminar. As for Beverly, she marveled at how much kids had changed since the fifties when they all knew where they were going, girls looking for husbands, boys pushing into starting positions, and now that all of those girls and boys were well over thirty-five, she wondered what all the push and struggle had gained them. They might have done better, Beverly thought, to graze in the pastures for a while like the State U. kids, to ask questions instead of taking other people's answers, and maybe even to suffer from the agonies of uncertainty and the consequences of risk, rather than rush into a race toward a finish line that was not, in the end, as glorious as they had been led to anticipate. Therefore, instead of being downcast and outcast among the youth of the seventies, Beverly had, in a way, regained her passport to a Greenwich Village of the spirit as she learned to live again among people who could see in history, art, literature, and loafing, realities as legitimate as house and family.

When Elliot Leighton, the English poet who had come for a year of teaching and writing in America, the land of opportunity, cocked his cauliflower ear toward the debate between Lars Hendersen and Beverly Gordon, he was paying far more than his ordinary, faint attention. Professor Leighton was a New-Style teacher: more interested in experience than knowledge, more eager to be intimate than authoritative. Afterwards, at Heightsville PTA meetings, Beverly the Parent would be able to argue with conviction that "learning" and "experience" are not the same thing. Beverly the Student, however, was lucky enough not to need solid information since she did not expect to be taking standardized tests or teaching future students of her own. She could sit back and enjoy the divertimentos of the poet-professor, who, at the impact of her response to Lars Hendersen's loaded question, had begun to look very wise and whimsical, like an owl with his nest overturned on his head, as he nodded in agreement.

"You're right, of course," he told the class at large in clipped Oxford English. Leighton had published five collections in the past seven years, so everyone admired him. "In poetry," he went on, "fucking must stand out as an extraordinary event. It demands any writer's utmost inventiveness. I remember in a ballad once I had a fellow caught in his trouser leg. Worked very well, that," he said, looking bacchic in his grape polo shirt. "After all"—he sighed like the west wind—"as

we all know"—he wiped his nose on his sleeve—"one fuck"—
he rolled his drunken-owl eyes—"gets to be very much like
another."

Before State U.—and her subsequent association with
shameless feminists—Beverly had been grossly underinformed
about sex. Her ignorance was blatant, as it would have been if
she had gone through school without instruction in American
history. Allison at ten years old had brought home from health
class a vocabulary that was news to Beverly, who wasn't even
sure—after her daughter's explanations—of the anatomical
geography it entailed. Beverly was the kind of person who
never really believed gossip. Neighborhood scandals seemed
as exotic and unreal as Jet Set activities. When either subject
arose in the chatter of the beauty parlor, Beverly was glad to
hide herself with a good book under the dryer.
Attribute her disinclination to the Lost Decade—the thirties or the twenties or whenever it happens that a woman's
head is down her children's throat with the freshly squeezed
orange juice, up their asshole with thermometers, into their
eyes and ears with educational toys, in the bathtub, in the
washing machine, the playground, the school. The Lost Decade when every good mother is as epicene as Mary Poppins
with her hands full and her head spinning, her uniform of
chopped hair, easy-care clothes, funny shoes, overweight, all
Mother Nature's way of keeping her daughters out of tempta-
tion's path and in line with generations of wonderful mothers
with beautiful children. So that for those crucial, family-
building years it was enough for Beverly, sexually speaking, to
be there, in the king-sized bed, to be spread out like a
gameboard whenever Peter Gordon was moved to play. And

if, sometimes, she actually felt like a gameboard or, worse, a board without a game, used and set aside, unchallenging, unchallenged, she had never expressed a complaint because she was always at least a little bit glad, relieved, grateful that a man as attractive as Peter wanted her at all. Only later, from revelations at women's Consciousness-Raising meetings, did she learn that she had less to complain about than many other family women, for she had not known (being so underinformed) that many men of Peter's age had begun to slow down, lose strength and interest. And later than that, when Beverly—a different woman—lay across a big brass bed that was like a movie set after a battle scene and thought about the barrely ribs and soft hands, the hairless testicles and the small feet of Harvey Porter, she could not help recalling Peter's dark and well-kept body, his heavy shoulders, flat hips that looked and felt lovely where the torso narrowed into the hard, effective pelvis with its jungle tangle of hair, and his long, well-shaped legs that so often had vined with hers. In the aftertimes, it was hard for Beverly to remember that before her son Sandy's Bar Mitzvah, which had marked the close of her Lost Decade, and before her emergence from the Bar Mitzvah depression to look for herself in college classrooms and on city streets, she had been a woman almost totally out of touch with sexuality beyond the routine of playing house in her decorated bedroom or an occasional chaste and filtered view on film or printed pages. Sex, like American history, was a subject of little appeal to Beverly, so she had not troubled herself to be educated. Like American history, the subject of sex had a threatening dark side and Beverly preferred to be comfortably ignorant. All of her life, she had accepted placid myths and avoided dangerous exploration. But as she reached out from her emotional darkness, the shock of new light and the fear of a return to darkness worked together to force her to stand up in the clear and face what was chasing her. It was then that Beverly painfully, inescapably, and triumphantly began to learn that regarding the subject of sexuality (as well as American history and everything else) truth may be terrifying but it is never so terrible as evasion.

Before she saw in the clear blue eyes of Harvey Porter that there was more to sex and American history than she had dreamed of, Beverly's closest brush with the possibility of extramarital adventure was the tentative and wistful suggestion of a classmate in Renaissance art, who fell in love with her because he thought she looked like Simone Signoret.

"You mean Simone Signoret now or Simone Signoret in *Room at the Top?*" she had asked him suspiciously.

Lew Chambertides—scholar, flute-player, admirer of the centrifugal battle scenes of Paolo Uccello—was an etiolated young man with the sparse beard and starved eyes of a portrait by his countryman El Greco. Beverly caught him staring at her and thought it was a tic or the mother thing again. Nothing he ever said in class made sense to her, and when the room was darkened for the showing of slides, she sometimes noticed him straining over a steno pad taking notes while everybody else was looking at the pictures. So on the day, not far into the spring term, when this odd person lingered by the classroom door while Beverly buttoned herself against the March cold, and skipped into step with her as she walked toward the student parking lot, she wondered what he might want: money? lecture notes? One compensation for her post–Bar Mitzvah misery had been the effortless loss of some twelve pounds and the concomitant development of a bustline. At one time she had feared that her baby fat would turn to middle-age spread with no intervening period of shapeliness. But thanks to anorexia, she had the best figure of her life since a few months in eighth grade after a summer at a nonsectarian scout camp where eating was a low priority. Even so, she did not expect college men to grow faint at the sight of her. Maybe, she thought, Lew Chambertides wanted a ride to his subway stop.

It was a cutting wind past the protection of the campus warren and Beverly ran among gusts of old snow while Lew Chambertides ran behind in a cloud of his own white breath. At the car, he suddenly took a knitted black hat from his pea-coat pocket and strapped it under his beard under his chin. So that when Beverly looked up from unlocking the driver's door, he was standing on the passenger side as solemn as an icon waiting to be let in. "Oh wow," he said when he had seated himself and begun to examine the dashboard and rub against the fake leather upholstery. "Some car," he said. Beverly, who usually sped back to Heightsville, commanded herself to sit still and wait. But only after she had turned on the motor, got the heater going, and waited some more did Lew Chambertides unsnap his little hat, fold it in half, put it back in his pocket, and say, his gaze striking about two inches above Beverly's eyes: "I'm very attracted to you." He wasn't at all good at lovemaking, he said, but he thought he might do better with Beverly. "I was turned on by you," he said, "from the first day with Giotto and Cimabue."

Beverly was very pleased and a little moved by his appeal. She thanked him sincerely.

"I didn't think you'd be interested," he said.

"I would be if I did that kind of thing. And I'm sure you'll get better with more experience. Everybody is slow at first." In the end, she drove him to his bus stop and they were still friends.

Lew left State U. after the spring term to join a crafts commune in Hamilton, Texas, and Beverly was intermittently sorry that she hadn't taken his offer. She was thirty-eight years old and she didn't look like a sexy French actress. She might, she reminded herself, never get another chance.

Not that age had to make a difference.

"You act like you're older," Joe Channing accused her.

Beverly: I *am* older.

Joe: Age doesn't signify. What signifies is people getting along. I'd be pissed off if you came on to me and said this dude's only twenty-two so I got to be like I'm with a kid.

Beverly: It's easy for you to say it, Joe, because you're the younger one. But if I started talking to you as a buddy and you decided I was some old bird trying to act young, you could put me down.

Joe: But don't you see, man? That would be *my* problem.

"No, mine," Beverly insisted. "I'm the sensitive one."

She had played that game before. In any category Joe could name. Having come to Heightsville from the city, where friendship had been instinctive and instantaneous; where last names were for doorbells and an address meant only where you went to see somebody. In the city, the question "What do you do?" might be answered "Ice-skate." The greatest concern over background was Bach versus soft jazz and would it interfere with conversation?

Fifteen years in Heightsville had changed Beverly's expectations. In a sad part of her memory there rolled a metaphoric film of her arrival one blooming June day, a fat Beverly smiling with the open eagerness of a newcomer to a block party (and bringing with her, of course, her contribution, a bubbling noodle pudding in a casserole dish under a napkin) and her reception, not with open arms but at arm's length by cool, tight-lipped ushers who put their fingers to their lips, showed her to her place, took the noodle pudding (with discreetly whispered thanks) out back someplace, and when it was time for refreshments to be served and everybody stood up and sidled out of their rows and filed down the aisles to line up at the thin table with sliced luncheon meat and three-bean salad and pale, flat cookies, Beverly already knew enough to talk in a whisper and put very little on her plate and not to ask what had happened to her bubbling, buttery noodle pudding, which was never seen again, the napkin and casserole dish never returned.

When Beverly moved to the pretty new house on the pretty old block in Heightsville, a new neighbor impetuously invited her to a membership tea at the Young Women's Club, learning too late that Beverly's straight nose and name were deceptive, for how could she, Tricia Hadley, be expected to recognize the difference between genteel and Gentile when nobody Jewish had ever lived on the block before? To rectify her error, she simply forgot to stop for Beverly on the afternoon of the tea, so that Beverly, dressed in her nicely-nicely pale blue coatdress and with a baby-sitter hired, waited and waited until she finally telephoned Tricia Hadley's house and learned that Tricia Hadley had left a long time earlier for her membership meeting at the Young Women's Club. Whether or not Tricia Hadley received Beverly's message is not clear, but Beverly certainly got hers, for Tricia Hadley never called again, either to apologize or explain, and she always managed to be across the street or down another supermarket aisle whenever she caught sight of Beverly first. And as if Tricia Hadley's lesson were not enough, Beverly learned more from her next-door neighbor Alicia Bradley, who stopped by one morning and stayed for coffee and examined the Gordons' furniture and pictures, curtains and carpeting as if she were memorizing them to tell the other neighbors and save them the trip; who came by on other occasions to borrow a cup of sugar or an Electrolux vacuum cleaner bag or to look at the obituary page in Beverly's New York *Times* or ask Beverly to sign for a United Parcel delivery; who chatted with her in the pleasant out-of-doors when they met wheeling strollers or carting groceries so that Beverly came to believe they were friends and invited Alicia Bradley and her husband to a small Saturday-night gathering with some of the Gordons' friends from the city, whereupon Alicia Bradley suddenly lost her focus, fell out of her sweet facial expression, and said flatly, "No, thank you," with such absence of echo or explanation that Beverly could see immediately that she had made another awkward mistake. And as if Alicia Bradley's lesson were not enough to make an indelible impression of the proper place for the Gordons, there was the further indicator of a broad study, which made it clear that during their first six months in Heightsville, the presentable, respectable, well-mannered, well-informed, good-mixing Gordons, having been continually invited out for cocktails, dinner, supper, Sunday brunch, and Saturday-afternoon wine tasting, had found themselves only in the homes of fellow Jews (though in many cases the Jews were not observant and in others only one side of the family was Jewish), so that when Beverly ended up sitting in the Heightsville library park with a squint-eyed, crazy-clean, child-worshipping, browbeating woman named Moskowitz who told her "I knew you and I were going to be the best of friends," Beverly finally, irrevocably caught on to the Big Idea of her rightful place in Heightsville, and from that time on her smile grew smaller and her elbows stayed closer in. And therefore she said to her young friend Joe Channing:

"If you want to be buddies, the first move has got to be yours."

And Joe Channing, who was black, felt sorry for Beverly and her peculiarities. "Look," Joe said. "An old broad comes on and lays a long rap on me, I think she's *boring*. Not *old*. You come on, you could be forty, it wouldn't make any difference."

And Beverly said, "That's good because in two years I'm going to be forty."

And Joe Channing said, "Oh Christ! Forty! I thought you were like twenty-nine!"

But they remained friends anyway.

Beverly had underestimated the power of youth to see through their fraudulent elders. Watching the respectful, receptive faces around the table in the Contemporary Poetry seminar, she was sure the students believed what Elliot Leighton was telling them. He told them that if everyone in the class would write one original poem a week, he would have all the poems published as a collection at the end of the term. "After all," he said, "my publisher owes me a favor, surely, since I never refuse to write a cheerful testimonial for his vile books by other authors." Mr. Leighton promised to write the preface himself and to divide the royalties among the class. "Perhaps my name on the cover," he said, rolling his eyes modestly, "will—as you Americans say—boost sales a bit."

Seeing their serious, listening faces, Beverly thought they were swallowing this nonsense as they seemed to swallow Mr. Leighton's inordinately flexible standards for the interpretation of contemporary poetry.

> Water opens without end
> At the bow of a ship
> Rising to descend
> Away from it
>
> Days become one
> I am who I was

"You really can feel the up and down of that water," Joe Channing said.

"Yeah. Yeah. I get that sense of traveling. I can really dig on it."

Tom Dalton, who was heavily into parapsychology, saw with his prophetic eyes how the universe was pulled together into the Great One, and Ivory Johnson, who was political, thought it was also about the oneness of people, "a kind of metaphoric integration poem," she said.

Lars Hendersen argued forcibly for its Freudian implications: the phallic ship cutting through the water, the water's rise and descent.

Paula Francese, teller of fortunes, saw only the Queen of Spades. "I think this poem is about death," she said.

Elliot Leighton agreed with them all. "Yes, quite," he told Paula. "One sees that clearly. The shadow pulling downward.

The cadence. The dying fall. Yes, very good."

Beverly saw him as a consumer fraud. She had grown up at the side of Sadie Peck, who stood in three-deep lines at delicatessen counters with her eyes on the scale and a finger pointed at the heart of the counterman. "Give me good weight!" Sadie Peck commanded and she got good weight and lean meat or else she was back at the counter that afternoon (Beverly beside her, melting away with embarrassment) but getting what she wanted and had paid for. Here was Elliot Leighton filling up his containers with more juice than coleslaw, tossing in pieces of not-so-fresh herring while these dopey kids who had not had the benefit of learning about life by shopping with Sadie Peck on Jerome Avenue sat politely and respectfully getting gypped. Beverly, who loved these dopey kids, worried about how they would get on in the world with no head for protecting themselves. She was not yet eight months removed from her son's Bar Mitzvah and she was still worrying about not getting taken, misled, used in the outside world. Joe Channing called it her shopping-bag morality. He told her she had a lot to learn, and not just contemporary poetry.

It felt strange to Beverly on Tuesday and Thursday afternoons, after Contemporary Poetry, when she stopped to do her dinner shopping in the Heightsville supermarket. On Tuesday and Thursday afternoons, everybody in Heightsville looked pastel. Walking from her car, she felt pangs of pluralistic societal schizophrenia as she fixed a bland face to meet her neighbors in a town where it was not considered at all irregular for a mature woman to leave a bridge table with the announcement that she was going to tinkle or for grown men to take the floor at monthly mayor-and-council meetings in public outcry against dog-do on the sidewalks. On Tuesday and Thursday afternoons, the Magic-Eye door of the airy, wide-aisled, odor-free supermarket flew open and drew Beverly back into the real world.

Peter was not happy with Beverly's decision to return to school.

"What do you need it for?" he had wanted to know. "If you expect to be a teacher, you could go to a teachers college. If you're looking for culture, you could go to museum lectures. But all this money just for graduate school? It's a waste."

Beverly thought of her birthday stocks, which lay under a press of papers at the bottom of a steel drawer behind a barred door in the back of the Heightsville Savings and Loan Company. She said, "I bet the accumulated interest on those stocks would pay for any classes I want to take."

She wants? She wants? What was this? Bubblehead Beverly asking for an accounting? She who was never interested enough even to open the envelopes with her quarterly dividends? Who endorsed the checks without even turning them over to see what they were? And now a confrontation, an accusation, a breakfast-table showdown over the four-slice electric toaster. The toast pops up and a bell rings in Beverly's head. "It isn't fair," she says, trying to look businesslike. "I always have to ask you for everything."

"Do I ever refuse you?"

"No. But I have to be grateful."

Peter didn't have time to argue. No matter who brought it in, the money went right out again. "We don't have yours and mine," he said. "It's all the same money. It's ours."

"Then I don't have to ask you about college, do I?"

"Go ahead," Peter said, all affection gone from his face.

More and more Peter had kept to himself, burrowing into his solitude, and the more he left her alone to walk solemnly around the edges of hers, the bitterer Beverly became, the more dissatisfied with him, and the less likely to respond when he turned to her in their king-sized bed with its custom-made spread folded neatly over the trouser stand.

"How can you expect me to love you at night," she demanded during a particularly jejune weekend, "after you've ignored me all day?"

"This is what I've always wanted," Beverly told Harvey Porter in his expense-account hotel room. "A beautiful one-shot deal. High talk and low sex and tomorrow goodby."

At "goodby" his eyes clouded. Beverly was ashamed. He was sitting in a red plush Wilton chair. She was cross-legged on the soft carpet with her head against his thigh.

"I guess," she said, "that since Sandy's Bar Mitzvah, I've been trying to break out of one frame or another." It was very late and she didn't want to be anywhere else, ever. Harvey stroked her hair that showed its gray in the dim lamplight.

"Breaking frames is not what life is about," Harvey said. "I believe it is more important to work with what's inside the frame, to improve on it and to repair it if necessary."

"Do you really think so?" She looked up into a face that surprised her. That Plymouth hardness had turned to a stubborn, fighting set that was almost frightening.

CHAPTER 7

Harvey Porter remembered when his older daughter Kitty was in Mr. Paul's class. It was the year that American history became the subject for supper-table talk. One evening, quite early in the school year, Kitty announced from her place at the kitchen table:

"That Hamilton was a rotten guy but I like him anyway."

"Hamilton who?" Sally sat very straight in her chair. She was pleased with Kitty's choice of topic. "What is it you like about him, dear?"

"I like the idea of a Bank of the United States and I also like his complete rivalry with Jefferson." Kitty knew she was

125

the brighter child. She was proud of her intelligence. She had a stern little face and a pale, downturned mouth. She turned expectantly to her father. "Did you know he called Jefferson the red-headed tombstone?"

Harvey had not been strictly attending. His head was someplace else, nowhere specific. He was in his middle forties. His fair hair was beginning to go gray. The slim, straight, almost delicate-looking body of his youth was meating out, which pleased him. He had a guilty feeling about himself, that he was frivolous, light-minded. He had wanted more severity. He believed that everybody had an age at which he was most properly himself. He thought his own right age would be fifty and he was working toward it. He had not been at his best as a youth: not carefree enough, awkward and too sensitive. Now, in whimsy that had a realistic center, he felt himself approaching an age at which he hoped the liabilities of his youth would become assets of a strong maturity.

"Jefferson?" He called himself to attention. "Oh. The red-headed tombstone," he said. "It wasn't only Hamilton who called him that, I'm afraid."

Suzy, two years Kitty's junior, began to lunge at her food with a fork in a clenched fist. It was one of her diversionary tactics and as usual it worked. Attention turned to her table manners.

Two years later, Suzy herself fell under the spell of Mr. Paul. Suzy was a bluejean girl, a T-shirt girl. Sneakers. Patches. She wore her hair long and straight and parted in the middle. She never sat upright, but sprawled, curled or slumped almost to her neck. She liked floors better than chairs, away better than home, friends better than schoolwork. So when Suzy began to talk history, it was a high tribute indeed to Mr. Paul's teaching skills.

Again at the supper table: "Did you know the Ku Klux Klan hung a black man upside down from a tree and somebody carved initials on his stomach?"

"Where did you hear that?" Sally liked the conversation to be wholesome. She organized suppers—always with protein, a starch, and a green vegetable or salad—so that hot foods were served from a heated electric tray and she could remain seated and contribute to the conversation. She always combed her hair and hung away her apron before taking her seat. Sally looked sharply at her husband as Suzy spoke.

"Mr. Paul told us a lot of stories about the KKK. He passed pictures around."

"Do you think that's going too far, Harve?"

"Some of the girls wouldn't look." Suzy tossed a quick glance to see if her ladylike sister was impressed. Kitty attended strictly to her lamb stew.

"They'd better look," Suzy's father said. "Because that's the way it was. And people had better look hard to make sure nothing like it ever happens again."

Mr. Paul had tight curls of red hair that stuck out like a ledge over his straight forehead, over his excited, humorous, and penetrating ice-blue eyes. He wore silver-rimmed glasses and his sharp cheeks had a permanent red shine. He was somewhere in his thirties, very small and agile, and he orchestrated his classes with tart authority.

Kids pulled their chairs into a circle and Mr. Paul, in a flared suit with one of his big bow ties, sat aloft on the back of a chair with his feet on the seat: waving his hands, pointing to this student and that, running question and answer games, moderating debates. He presented historical dramas in which he played all the parts himself. Sometimes students did the role playing. Sometimes he stood, immobile, at the blackboard and simply battered material into their heads. But even Suzy Porter, who dreamed through other classes, sat up straight for Mr. Paul, who would not put up with slouching. She spoke clearly because Mr. Paul marked down for sloppy enunciation and bad grammar—no *likes*, *you knows*, *I means*—and, if he were in a particularly cranky mood, also for sloppy appearance. So Suzy Porter, like the other students, rose to Mr. Paul's demands.

The kids took it for granted that he was queer. He wasn't married. Or engaged. He lived up in Hartford and the kids giggled about his living arrangements because if they happened to need to telephone him about an assignment or some business of the journalism club, sometimes the roommate answered. This assumption made no difference at all. Mr. Paul was the best social studies teacher that anyone could remember having been taught by in the Waddingford Junior High School. Ten minutes of Friday class was given over to student questions, with a reward—a candy bar or cookie—for stumping the teacher. But though they got together in groups on Thursday afternoon and conferred by telephone all Thursday night, the kids could seldom find a fact that was new to Mr. Paul.

"Don't be distressed," he comforted them after he had told them who had lost to Herbert Hoover in 1928 and why. "The people in my evening college class, some of whom are graduate students, are also losing their minds trying to stump me. I feel a bit sorry for them because they're older and they work very hard at it. Sometimes I hesitate and pretend to be caught, so they won't feel like complete pushovers. They're really down when I get the answer. But they keep trying."

He pursed his lips and leaned closer to his class, his eyes and cheeks shining. "For you people," he said in mock confidence, "there is no hope. You might as well give up."

But they never did.

And many of them, when they'd gone on to college and been there awhile, came back to visit Mr. Paul and thank him.

When Jonathan Paul got into trouble, his students didn't know what to think. Warren Hamisch, the owner of the Waddingford Pharmacy, a slow-moving man who had a friendly word for everyone in town, spoke for many parents when he said that Mr. Paul had no right to be teaching adolescent children. And Mr. Hamisch was the president of the Waddingford Board of Education.

The eighth-graders, who looked up to Mr. Hamisch and who still believed in their parents, didn't know what to think.

The Waddingford weekly picked up the article from the Hartford daily: a Gay Liberation conference and rally had been held at the Eastside Unitarian Church in Hartford. One of the afternoon panels—on the subject of "Emerging from the Closet: When, Where, How, and Mostly Why"—had been conducted by Jonathan Paul, Ph.D., teacher of social studies and vice-president of the Gay Activist Alliance of Hartford County. The Waddingford weekly was tossed on or somewhere-in-the-vicinity-of doorsteps late on Wednesday afternoon.

It was a small item on a page that was almost entirely given over to weekend food specials at a local butcher's and grocery store. It appeared on a pleasant day in early May when the town seemed to be especially quiet, from the broad white houses along Main Street to the rows of Cape Cods out by the paper works, all in a hush perhaps not to disturb the roses which were budding in front yards or the rapidly leafing trees. But gradually, after the delivery, house by house and block by block, figures slipped out of doorways and across lawns, cars backed out of garages, telephones began to ring, there was movement in the town. And by suppertime there was scandal. That very night the Waddingford Board of Education called an informal meeting at Warren Hamisch's house and all six members, for once, attended. The Superintendent of Schools showed up halfway through and ten minutes later telephoned Mr. Macomber, the principal of the Waddingford Junior High School, who was there almost immediately. On Thursday morning, before classes began, Jonathan Paul was summoned to the principal's office.

Mr. Macomber was a youngish man, younger than Mr. Paul, but much less alive. His thin, tan hair was combed back to expose the encroaching V's of baldness and his eyes were like marbles. He talked in a toned-down, unvarying voice, often in terms of "input" and "outreach." He stood behind his desk as Jonathan Paul knocked, entered, waited cheerfully. Paul was wearing a blue bow tie with yellow butterflies. A claret-colored blazer. He always stood as if he were ready to spring up like a jack-in-the-box. Macomber, in a brown suit, seemed to hang from his own square shoulders. He didn't sit down, so his visitor didn't sit down. Macomber showed Paul the clipping from the Waddingford weekly. "I don't know if you've seen this yet."

Paul glanced at it and nodded. He hadn't seen it but he had expected it.

"Is there a mistake?" Macomber asked in mechanical syllables. "Is this you?"

"No question." It had been only a few months since he had become an officer. He had been a member of GAAHC for over two years. Each forward step he had taken had been weighted down by considerable turmoil. The physical fear of taking risks. The mental agony of making risky decisions.

The principal looked at him curiously, possibly with contempt as well as curiosity behind his cold eyes. "There is no arguing about taste," he said. "Your private life is your own."

Mr. Paul stood still, still just inside the closed door. Waiting.

"But flaunting it in public is a different matter."

Mr. Macomber moved a few papers around. Input. Output. He preferred to deal with papers. He preferred remote control. Looking toward Mr. Paul, he looked bleak.

"We can't afford to lose good teachers." This he put as a rebuke, his first hint of anger or dismay. But he caught himself immediately. He said he was sorry but he would have to remove Mr. Paul from the classroom situation. "I'm under orders, you know," the principal said, making a helpless, angry gesture with his hands.

Jonathan Paul was not shocked. He had expected an upheaval sooner or later, ever since he decided to affirm himself and exercise his rights as a citizen, and really—in all honesty—to assert his rights and other people's rights as public school teachers. But he was surprised that Mr. Macomber found it necessary to accompany him to his classroom and watch from the doorway as he collected his belongings, then usher him to the parking lot door and stay there, too, watching till Mr. Paul had driven safely away from school. It was a little

bit demeaning, that. It all happened quickly, before the start
of the school day. Only a few students saw. The substitute
hadn't arrived yet. But Mr. Paul felt, as he was meant to feel,
humiliated.

Harvey Porter had a small, three-room office over an
antique shop in a second-string shopping center just outside
Waddingford. It was functional and comfortable. A part-time
typist-receptionist had the front room, which was also a waiting room, rarely crowded. Porter had a consultation room
with his own desk and files. And he had a "library," a room
that was heavy with books, with a long conference table that
was a study in rectangles—open lawbooks, neatly piled docu-
ments, yellow pads for notes, letters neatly arranged for quick
reference—at which he liked to work standing up. He was
there, in his library, his workroom, standing erect, deep in
work, in a white shirt and dark necktie, his mind in a lawbook,
when the call came. Of course he remembered Jonathan Paul.
Porter had visited his class once, when Kitty was in Junior
High, to give a talk about civil liberties. Porter was still in law
school at the time. He'd done it again, though, just the year
before, when Suzy was in Mr. Paul's class.

"Specifically, what happened?" he asked Mr. Paul, as if he
had just been thinking about him.

"Are you upset?" was the next thing he wanted to know.
"Do you want to come right up and talk about it?"

"Thanks muchissimo," Mr. Paul said. He was going to
hole up for the day and pull himself together. "I'm not panick-
ing," he said. They made a date for early next morning.

"I'll be glad to see you," Harvey Porter said. And he *was*
glad. It was good to be doing something instead of just talking

about it. He had always been somewhat contemptuous of himself and doubtful of his motives. He felt better having experienced the outflow of sincerity with which he responded to Jon Paul's call for help. He felt pretty good about himself in the days that followed. If Sally had reservations, she kept them to herself. As for the girls, of course they fairly danced with enthusiasm. Mr. Paul was a hero of theirs. Now their father was about to become a hero, too.

The first thing Harvey Porter did was protest to the State Commissioner of Education, who quickly ruled that Mr. Paul could not be suspended without pay unless he was shown, somehow, to be doing harm to his students. Quickly, too, Mr. Paul was unsuspended but given a significant change of assignment: he was to work at a desk in the administration wing of the school building, far from the young people, as some kind of public relations assistant, to write short essays about the accomplishments of the Waddingford school system. He was not to use school corridors. He was not to have lunch in the school cafeteria. Before he could return to the classroom, he was to take a psychological examination to prove himself fit to associate with, let alone instruct, teen-age youngsters.

Porter protested again and recaptured Mr. Paul's right to the convenience and subsidized prices of the cafeteria, which by law served all students and school employees who wanted to eat there.

He reclaimed Mr. Paul's right to use the halls and toilets of the school in which he worked.

He also established that it was the duty of the Superintendent of Schools to see that Mr. Paul had meaningful work to do during the hours for which he was paid and until he could return to the work he had been trained and hired to do.

All of these rulings were won with dispatch by letter or personal appearance within six weeks of the publication of the controversial news story. But the order for a psychological test stuck, though Harvey Porter appealed to state authorities and continued to appeal all through the summer.

It was a difficult point: Mr. Paul, through his lawyer, contended that the local board must produce concrete evidence that there was reason to believe him harmful to students. The board, on its side, had managed to produce a letter from a psychiatrist who practiced in New Haven which suggested that a member of a homosexual organization could, by example, put an imprimatur on sexual deviance. And so the case was stalled at the end of the school year: Mr. Paul on the payroll, out of the classroom; the board awaiting the results of a psychological test which they hoped would justify the teacher's summary dismissal; Harvey Porter appealing, on Mr. Paul's behalf, an order which he considered to be a violation of the personal and political rights of teachers.

Harvey Porter had spent most of his life in small towns, but he was not altogether provincial. Nobody had to explain to him the rock-bottom base of the outcry against Jon Paul. It was in the teacher's popularity, his downright acceptability. It was one thing, Harvey Porter explained to Sally during one of their strolls in the fragrance of a June evening, to be a female impersonator, to simper and posture, and play up to the pubescent jocks, as, for example, Fred Gallegher, the guidance counselor, was laughingly reputed to do. All the kids were on to Gallegher. They made jokes to his face, according to Suzy, and Gallegher laughed with them.

"Fred Gallegher plays the freak," Harvey said, as they

turned to go up their long driveway. "He knows his place and nobody minds him."

But Jonathan Paul was no freak.

He was a man his students could admire.

A man like Mr. Paul could make homosexuality seem acceptable.

And so he was dangerous.

Harvey Porter was aware of the depth of the problem.

Mr. Paul kept up his outward insouciance at some emotional expense. He didn't like being an example. He didn't like that kind of attention. It didn't do his nervous system any good. He vomited almost every night. Most mornings he awoke with the sunrise and between dream and daylight, taunted by the squawks of bluejays, unable to sleep, unwilling to rise, he was visited by swarming and jangling phantasms of disgrace, humiliation, destruction. He lay in a sweat most mornings from six o'clock till seven, when it was time to get up, take a shower, and turn on the morning news. One of the few thoughts that comforted him was that Harvey Porter was on his side: Porter, a family man, an elder of the Presbyterian church, a member of the Drug Abuse Committee and the Committee for Clean Air and Clear Water. Harvey Porter was at his side and was, if ever there was one, a solid citizen. This was real support.

After the relief of a distant, rambling, unworried summer during which he had managed to escape the problems of acceptance and rejection, Mr. Paul returned in September to resume his fight in Waddingford. The appeal still pending, he returned to the administration wing. Harvey Porter decided to appeal directly to the local board for a classroom assignment. He thought he had a way to make it happen.

On the first Tuesday of the month, the Waddingford Board of Education met in open session. A large attendance anticipated, they used the meeting room in the Waddingford Public Library and they started at seven-thirty, a half hour earlier than usual. It looked like church at Easter, the way people piled up the green-lined path from Main Street to the pillared porch of the library, an old white frame building, beautifully kept, like the other great old houses, too big for modern families, that had been transformed to house the Waddingford Elks and the Waddingford Mental Health Clinic. The heavily leafed elm trees made a dark outside ceiling between the town and the sky. Inside the library, light from the brass wall sconces shone gold on the beeswaxed, plank floor of the broad front hall. In the meeting room, where recessed white lights supplemented the glow of the teardrop chandelier, the rows of folding chairs were filled by the time the routine reports were read. People were standing along the back wall, up the side aisles. The reporter from the local weekly counted forty-eight present. The Hartford daily set the attendance at sixty-five.

Mr. Paul, looking older with his glasses on, but still ruddy and dapper in a striped blazer with a solid four-in-hand instead of his customary bow tie, sat at the end of the fourth row beside his friend and lawyer, Harvey Porter. Porter was in a dark suit, prosperous-looking, easily correct. His soft, pale hair was graying and his handsome, strong-boned face was creased with lines of concentration. When he took his seat, during the early proceedings, a few board members, including the board president himself, had looked up from their notes, turned in their chairs at the long mahogany table to greet him, Hamisch, the president, even calling out, "Evening, Harve," as if they were meeting at a Little League game.

"Hello there, Warren," Porter had returned, as if they had not been sparring by mail, by telephone, and in face-to-face engagements for almost four months. Hamisch was a soft, slow-motion man with a tuft of black hair and small eyes in a hearty face. He was, in daily life, an easygoing, likable neighbor and his pharmacy a favorite meeting place.

Harvey Porter at that psychological moment would ordinarily have clapped his client on the shoulder, a reassuring gesture and a show of solidarity. But he felt a physical constraint. He knew what earnest and hard work went into the committee reports he was hearing. He knew the people who were reading them and the people who were listening; most of them were people he liked, his friends, friends of Sally's, people they did business with. He hoped he could show them, reasonably, that a teacher's right to belong to an unpopular organization simply had to be respected. Porter, himself reasonable, understood their opposition though he did not sympathize with it. What would the board do, he had asked Warren Hamisch at a summer party where both were guests, if a teacher became an officer of a women's rights group or a champion of low-cost housing in a one-acre zone? Would those teachers be dismissed? Hamisch had laughed with him but said nothing.

Porter had not pressed his point. Even their correspondence had been carried on in a chummy, corner-store way. The board members had secretly rejoiced upon learning that Porter was to represent Mr. Paul. Harve Porter was, they knew, at bottom, one of them, an old townsman. They could depend on him.

So when Old Business had dragged on to the point of incoming mail and it was time to read the letter from the State Commissioner ordering Mr. Paul to be retained at full pay until the board should act on the results of a psychological test, nobody was really very excited to hear Harvey Porter's letter arguing, first, that membership in the GAAHC did not designate a person as homosexual any more than membership in the NAACP made him a Negro; and, second, that since, according to a recent ruling by the American Psychiatric Association, homosexuality was not to be classified as a mental disorder, the board order for psychological testing was inappropriate and clearly being used as a weapon for harassment and intimidation of a teacher who had embarrassed the system.

The board made a brief reply.

Declaring that Mr. Paul's "visibility" in the Gay Activist movement had "evidenced a harmful, significant deviation from normal mental health and affected his ability to teach, discipline, and associate with students," the board reissued its order for testing.

In fact, Mr. Paul would have welcomed the chance to take tests he was sure would prove him both sane and competent to teach. But he had more faith in people than his lawyer did. "Never admit you are homosexual," Porter kept telling him. "That is your most important holding. That's where we've got them." Porter wanted to win this case without giving an inch. He wanted to fight it on solely political ground, on the constitutional question of freedom of expression. "I know that you respect yourself," Harvey Porter assured his client. "But just for the moment, don't make any statements. Let's keep the issue clear."

So Jonathan Paul sat forward with his elbows on his
knees, and his sharp, ruddy face propped up by a thumb under
his chin. And Harvey Porter sat back, impassive and attentive,
as Warren Hamisch lit up a pipe and began to call for com-
ments and questions from the floor.

A woman in tweed stood to read from a slip of paper:

"Most parents would not choose to put their children in
the care of a homosexual or a person who advocated the acceptance of homosexuality as normal. Most parents cannot
afford to send their children to private school but do pay taxes
to support public schools. Therefore, since the state requires
children to be educated and since parents have no reasonable
choice outside of public schools, then it is up to the state to
hire teachers who are acceptable to the parents.

"When a school board retains the services of an advocate
of homosexuality, it places minority rights above majority
rights."

Porter knew her. She and her husband operated a laun-
derette and self-service dry cleaner out on the highway. They
had small children.

"Who will next be presiding over our classrooms?
Thieves? Prostitutes? Drug peddlers?"

She earned a little extra money by working at the polls on
registration and election days.

Harvey Porter wondered who had written her speech. If
Jonathan Paul was stricken, he managed not to show it.

Warren Hamisch pointed to a short, fierce-looking old
man, carefully dressed. He was a retired grain salesman. His
message was short after the requisite announcement of name
and address:

"We are wasting time, to say nothing of taxpayers' money,

by being forced to pay this deviant person a full wage when we no longer want him, or need him in the school."

Harvey knew him well. Always outspoken, usually irate, he harped on the tax problem. Again understandably, as he and his wife lived on a fixed income that covered them more narrowly with every passing year.

A small, dark man in a short-sleeved shirt spoke next. He looked foreign-born and Harvey didn't know him. He probably came from one of the houses out by the paper works. "Do you have to wait for him to be caught molesting somebody before you get rid of him?"

Harvey wished he had been able to persuade his client to stay away. He wished again that he could put out a hand to comfort him. This was an unusual night for Waddingford. Usually people were not so blunt, so stirred up. That was not at all the Waddingford style. If people had complaints, they usually came at them around corners and on padded feet. Direct attack was most unusual.

At last a young man was recognized, who Harvey knew would be on the right side. Jeff Myer, with a drooping western moustache and a cowboy's lean slouch, had once been an admirer of Kitty Porter. He gave as his current address a midwestern university. He read from a typewritten paper:

"Mr. Paul is a competent teacher, highly regarded by his students and fellow faculty members. There is no evidence that he sought to inject his political beliefs into his teaching or that he tried to influence his students." Jeff folded his slip of paper and moved out to the aisle where he could see everybody. Then he continued:

"If a person doesn't have the full approval of the society he lives in, does he lose his right to fight for what he believes

in? Or do we have free speech here? I learned more in Mr.
Paul's class than in all my other classes in Waddingford
schools. And not about homosexuality either."

There was some applause after Jeff's speech, mostly from
young people. Marilyn Jonas, the valedictorian, the previous
year, of Waddingford High, spoke next:

"We would all be against misconduct." She was dark and
intense. "But an individual must be judged or evaluated by his
conduct, not by his sex. Mr. Paul was my teacher and he was
one of the most learned, most interesting teachers I ever had
and one of the most honest, understanding, and open human
beings I ever met.

"There is no reason to believe that a homosexual teacher
will have a more adverse effect on students than a heterosex-
ual teacher. Teachers do not usually discuss their private lives
in the classroom." She obviously intended to say more, but
could not go on. She suddenly dropped into her chair and
covered her face. Mr. Paul moved toward her, but Harvey
Porter restrained him. Marilyn had calmed herself by the time
the next speaker began. He was George Bennett, a member of
the Town Council's library committee, a former New Yorker,
the retired curator of the Museum of the American Indian, a
thin, dry man with heavy white eyebrows. He spoke hesitantly:

"Perhaps if these defenders of the First Amendment were
parents of a teen-age boy, they might see things differently.
They might not be so eager to place a Mr. Paul in a position to
exert, even inadvertently, an influence on that boy, which
might set the pattern for the rest of his life."

Another man, Porter's dentist, always of strong political
opinion, was on his feet, without waiting to be recognized. He
was a bald, hollow-chested man with a nose like a toucan. He

was wearing a denim suit, newly fashionable that year. He spoke angrily but with weighty conviction: "The source of homosexuality is as much a mystery as why some people are black and others white. Psychiatrists know only that sexual identity is set at a very early age. Under kindergarten age. For a teacher to change that identity is about as likely as his making a white person black by teaching about Marcus Garvey, Harriet Tubman, and Crispus Attucks."

Harvey Porter had to smile. Gus Abbott was right as usual and as always a firebrand, always with the underdog. Which Mr. Paul assuredly was, with few other than former students ready to take his part. No teacher, Harvey noticed sadly, had spoken up, even though all of the teachers' right of expression was involved here. But he couldn't blame them either. They had jobs to protect. Nobody wanted to lose favor with the authorities. And yet Porter, no less than Mr. Paul, was astounded by the force of the animosity. By the time Warren Hamisch was summing up the board consensus, Mr. Paul had come to understand that many parents who had liked him, been grateful to him and friendly toward him without ever having imagined him to be a family man, certainly aware that he was not straight as a die, were now solidly behind the board's attempt to get rid of him.

"The board," Warren Hamisch said, "is fulfilling its mandate when it seeks to remove a school employee whom it finds to have a negative effect on the students."

Harvey Porter at last raised a hand and stood to address his fellow townspeople. He had spoken in this and in other meeting rooms many times before, more often from the platform than from the floor and always in support of a popular issue: clean air, good education, a youth-counseling center to combat a growing drug problem. So the people in town gave him respectful attention and he knew his words would have weight.

"Mr. Hamisch—my friend Warren, here—worries about the effect on our young people if a teacher reputed to be homosexual is permitted to remain on the staff. I don't worry about that. Mr. Paul has been teaching here more than successfully, for—what is it?—eight years? He hasn't changed. He's the same person he was last year and all those other years, except maybe even smarter because he, like all the rest of us, I hope, is learning all the time."

He talked slowly and simply. No one could question his sincerity. And the townspeople kept listening, knowing that he represented Mr. Paul, but knowing also that Harve Porter was no radical and would surely work out some compromise that would leave the town feeling clean.

"Mr. Hamisch believes that keeping Mr. Paul's services would somehow validate homosexuality in the eyes of some students and would also look like an endorsement by the board of deviant sexual behavior.

"Neither point is honestly arguable. All it means when a board hires or retains a teacher is that he or she is thought to be a competent professional. I would like to see Jonathan Paul back in his classroom, back running the journalism club at the Junior High School by, say, Thursday morning of this week. The board can take a vote right this minute. There are no legal grounds to keep him out. There are no moral grounds unless we're at the old game of punishing people for having different ideas from ours."

There was applause from the young people and from some of the adults, even from some of the antagonists who appreciated Harve Porter's gentle and conciliating tone. Members of the board leaned together and whispered among themselves until Warren Hamisch rapped his gavel.

"There will be no decision tonight. We're waiting for a state ruling about a psychological test. Naturally, we'll do what the state tells us to and we hope, of course, that it will be agreeable to Mr. Paul. I'd like to remind my good friend Mr. Porter that the board serves as representative of the community. We have a responsibility that I think all of us take very seriously, very gravely. All we try to do is to reflect majority opinion in the way our schools are run. We try to remember that the schools belong to the people."

Harvey Porter looked around at all the straight, white American faces of the people who were now applauding for Warren Hamisch. *Power to the people*, he thought ironically. All depends, doesn't it? he thought, on what people you're talking about. It was a fine little town for the people who lived in it. Only an undercurrent of guilt pulled him back from completely enjoying his position here. He had assuaged his cantankerous conscience by entering the law, and by practicing diligently, being fair about fees and generous with time and effort. And he had become, in recent years, an accepted liberal in this conservative town.

But he saw now that, like Jonathan Paul, he would be acceptable only as long as he did not act on his beliefs. So long as he did not present any real threat of change, he could say what he liked. He could preach idealism like a priest at a sacrament. Everyone would offer an easy amen. He had assuaged his guilt with talk and kept himself comfortable.

He walked with Mr. Paul to the teacher's little red Triumph parked around the corner on High Street. Mr. Paul was in a hurry to get home and find some comfort. Porter

walked slowly back to the library to wait for Warren Hamisch.
When Hamisch finally came down the path, one of the last to
leave, Porter met him on the sidewalk. They stood on Main
Street, in the light of a street lamp. They looked like two
friends passing the time, but Hamisch saw metal in the
lawyer's eyes.

"If Mr. Paul is not immediately reinstated as a classroom
teacher, I promise you that he will publicly confess to being a
practicing homosexual."

Hamisch listened, not understanding.

"If this happens," Porter went on, "the Waddingford
Board of Education will be accused of punishing him for the
practice of sodomy, which, I might remind you, is no longer
against the law in this state if it is practiced in private by two
consenting adults. If the question of sodomy arises, we will
have a demonstration in Waddingford. I am ready for it. So is
Mr. Paul and a network of Gay Activist groups. If a question of
sodomy arises, we are going to have another Scopes trial here.
Every Gay Activist in the state and a good many from the rest
of the country will be camping out in our parks and demon-
strating on our streets.

"If your majority wants its children protected from Mr.
Paul, I think they will be unhappy with the presence of some
of the more colorful members of the Gay Liberation movement, who will be more than willing to turn our town into one
of the circuses of the century.

"This will happen, Warren, as soon as Mr. Paul identifies
himself as a practicing homosexual. Otherwise, we have a
simple First Amendment case here, which I have persuaded
Mr. Paul to limit himself to for the sake of the community. . . . You have till Monday to get him back in class."

Warren Hamisch stood very still, and very painfully let

out his breath. Harvey Porter remembered that he always let schoolchildren use the bathroom in back of his store. "I see," Hamisch said finally. "I can't believe you're doing this to us."

The two men stood, with the light on them, on a strip of sidewalk between the smooth lawn and the spiky, grass-tufted shoulder of Main Street. A sharp September rain had begun to fall, gentled by the thickly leafed elm trees. That is the mistake that principled people make, Harvey thought. They behave with civility, avoid stepping on toes. When force is the only way to get things done. He caught the dismay on Hamisch's face and the rising anger. He turned away without much joy. He did not relish victory by bludgeon.

Late Friday night there was a shriek between the twin beds of Sally and Harvey Porter. Sally, waking first, recognized the telephone and woke Harvey to pick it up.

It was Lieutenant Giordano at the police station.

"Oh Lord!" Sally switched on the reading lamp. Where were the girls? What time was it?

"It's all right," Harvey said, still listening to the policeman. Suzy was all right. No car accident. The kids were all fine. Just the usual. Marijuana. Would they come down to the station for her?

It was almost one o'clock. They'd been unusually tired, both of them, and had gone to bed early, leaving the front door unlocked for the girls. Kitty was a senior and could stay out as late as she pleased, within reason. Suzy was expected to be home before midnight. Sally felt terrible. Suzy had just started this late partying, just since the summer. Sally should have waited up for her.

All the time, she was hurrying into her clothes. Girdle.

Stockings. Loafers to match her skirt. It wouldn't do to turn up looking ragged. She buttoned her blouse, thoughts colliding. "Are you wearing just a polo shirt, Harve? Don't wear the jacket with the stain. I've got to take it to the cleaner."

She knew Suzy had not taken drugs.

It was being done, but not by the Porter girls. Sally had told them time and again about the importance of keeping in control of oneself. By example, she and Harvey had taught the girls to respect themselves, their mind and body.

He went downstairs. She heard him backing out the car. She rushed down, taking a fast look in the hall mirror, seeing a comely woman who had not been aroused from sleep, who was not worried about her child, whose husband was not going through some kind of identity crisis, and who would not be discomfited in a police station. But she also saw her leather-gloved hand tremble so that it could not turn the doorknob without the other hand to steady it.

Harvey had had a few drinks that night and it was taking his head some time to clear. He stood for a moment in front of the red brick police station, part of a squat building that also housed the fire department and most municipal offices. He pulled in several deep breaths and said to his wife, who was standing beside him, light with uncertainty, "Maybe you'd rather wait in the car?" Her answer was to walk ahead of him into the building. He followed, trying to get his armor back.

Five teen-agers were standing in a dim corner of the reception room, Suzy among them. There were two policemen at the desk, one on the radio to patrol cars, one pecking at a manual typewriter. A flashing amber signal from the traffic light outside washed through the glass doors and across the tile floor, hitting the unblinking glow of the red exit light over the door to the back room. The ceiling was high and the walls were dark. The five teen-agers looked small.

Sally asked at the desk for Lieutenant Giordano. Harvey hurried to put his arms around his daughter. She pulled away from him. "Are you all right?" She didn't want to be a baby. "What's up, Suzy?" She put her face into his chest and started to cry. Lieutenant Giordano came out of the back room. Sally ran to him at the door. She said, "There must be a mistake."

The other four youngsters regrouped to exclude Suzy and her father. None of them looked at him. Heads down, all of them. Shoulders hunched. Hands in pockets. They pulled close together.

The lieutenant had a Baggie, a Saran Wrap bagful of guilty choppings. Thirty grams of marijuana found in Suzy's shaggy pouch of a handbag. Enough for judicial proceedings.

"Is it yours?" her father asked her.

Suzy shook her head. Her freckled face was pale and spotted in the red-and-yellow light. She was short and she had long hair. She was in bluejeans and a Donald Duck shirt. She was a young fifteen. "I was holding it for somebody," she said. "I really was. I hope you believe me."

"Of course we believe you, dear," Sally said loud enough for everybody to hear her.

Harvey had questions. Where were these kids? Where did the police find them? Why did they look in Suzy's bag? He wanted to know the circumstances.

Lieutenant Giordano was busy. Other parents had arrived, a disheveled couple bursting in to reclaim a gangling son in a WJHS jacket. Another father with uncombed hair and a pajama shirt under his unbuttoned topcoat had collared another boy and pushed him to the desk, then through the doorway to the back room. The two remaining youngsters huddled tight together. Lieutenant Giordano turned back to Sally and Harvey. "Let's just get these kids home," he said. "We had to book your daughter. It's the law, you know. Any questions you'll have to take up with Captain Pickett in the morning. Or with Judge Devlin."

There was nothing more for Harvey to say.

They passed another set of parents getting out of their car in front of the station. Suzy was looking up at her father with her heart in her eyes. "I can't tell you whose it was. Not one of my close friends. Not a real friend at all. This person just asked me to hold it and I couldn't say no.

"They asked me because I'm never in trouble. They said nobody would look in my bag. Everybody knows I don't smoke pot."

"Is that true?" Harvey asked. It was important to know. "Do you occasionally take a puff with your friends?" He looked into her eyes. "Just once in a while?"

Suzy hesitated.

"Of course she doesn't!" Sally cried. "Suzy wouldn't do that to us."

Harvey supposed that the police knew who were the drinkers and who the potheads. The police had a better than fair idea of what went on at Waddingford house parties and in the parking lot behind the Kool-Fresh ice-cream stand. In Waddingford—he smiled ruefully to himself—there was no need for spying and dossiers. A person could be got at. Oddly, it had not been long ago that he talked to his daughters, each separately, about drugs, his disapproval, his expectation that his daughters were sound enough to stay clear, yes, even of marijuana. Suzy had referred pointedly to his drinking. He had stood on the ground of the illegality of pot. It did seem really execrable to him. So young, these kids.

Porter made a few careful visits early the next morning, before he went to the police station. There was no help. Possession of thirty grams of marijuana meant juvenile court and—should a judge choose to be inordinately severe—sentencing to a juvenile detention institution. In any case, there would be a scandal and, despite legal niceties, probably a record. Harvey Porter simply could not take chances with his daughter. He didn't discuss the matter with Sally. He went to Warren Hamisch. The following week, Mr. Paul began to look for a job in another part of the state, in a private school.

Harvey Porter was wrenched by the feeling that God had punished him for his arrogance. He knew this was a primitive feeling, for he did not believe in a punishing God. Yet he was humbled and stunned by the depths of his townspeople's vengefulness. Suzy was out of trouble: nothing on the book, she and her friends clean as new. Porter's pride had gone before the fall.

Waddingford soon began to turn red and orange with leaves on the trees and leaves on the ground. He kept himself busy raking, piling them high, and burning them. Often over a late nightcap, he thought back through the events of early September and tried to see how he might have handled things differently.

"Why don't your daughters like you?"

"I may have been too strict with them when I was younger. They may have found me remote and unfeeling."

"How could that be? You're a man anybody can talk to."

"I wish that were true, that I could talk easily. And laugh easily."

Beverly's incredulity saddened him. But he kept his eyes on her. "I have difficulty even now," he admitted. "My daughter Kitty telephones every month or so. She talks with her mother. Then I get on. Kitty continues to chatter and to give me her news. But there is a sharp edge in her voice. She talks in a way that cuts me out. It's hard to explain but there is a forced gaiety in her voice that sets up a wall between us. Then I feel guilty that I can't get through to her. Maybe I don't try hard enough."

"Maybe you try too hard," Beverly said.

Harvey Porter was at the end of his line. Where was his future? He had been produced by memorable generations of often illustrious Americans. Porters had joined colonies, fought in the Revolution, founded banks, negotiated annexations, endowed colleges, collected art. The family had been full of Harvey John Porters and John Harvey Porters numbering into IIs, IIIs, and IVs. Harvey's grandfather had lost a fortune. Harvey's father, suddenly without support, had quit college, taken lowly work, and married beneath himself. As children, Harvey and his older brother had sat at a spare dining table and eaten in silence while their parents talked about produce from out back. Harvey's parents had talked about beans and lettuce just as Beverly's parents, in much greater tonal variety, had talked about prices at the delicatessen. Harvey was a good boy, sustained by praise for staying clean and playing quietly, not fighting with his brother, not talking out of turn. For his containment he received widespread approval. And in case the power of tacit discipline failed, he was also taught that ugly thoughts, angry words, and selfish deeds would earn him the wrath of a punishing God. He was taught to do his duty.

"It's tough to be a Wasp," Beverly agreed.

But on the other hand, he had not brought up his daughters to be Jewish. He had brought them up as he had been brought up but with diminishing conviction. Now he was at the end of his line, a dying branch on a tall tree. His girls were no longer Porters. They showed no interest in continuance. His grandson's name was Bruce Czajkoski.

"My daughters have felt the untruth of my life," Harvey confessed. "I became a set of good manners with a mirrored wall, a continual questioning of the carrying out of my everyday acts. Did I err? Suffer for it. Err and suffer became circular. Naturally, I was inaccessible. My daughters were forced to deal, as was everyone else in my circle, with my manners and my conscience. My daughters wanted more than that and never got it."

The walls of the round room contracted and Beverly felt herself bleeding from his wounds. She had no vocabulary for pain. She had learned only the words for pleasure.

"If you couldn't, you couldn't and that was you," she said. "Not everybody can lay himself out on a table. It doesn't make you a criminal."

She talked into his eyes, herself laid out. "It may be only that you feel guilty about it and the girls are feeding off your guilt. As a special favor to you."

She laughed at herself. A psychologist. Harvey's situation took shape in her mind as clearly as a case history. She could never figure out her own troubles, and her own pain was as remote as a poverty pocket in an affluent society. But Harvey listened to her. He thought she might be right. He saw how he might rearrange the pieces in a Father-Daughter guilt game.

"Pull back," Beverly said. As she said it, a tight cap slipped off from under her headskin and made her feel congenially light. "Pull back," she said, seeing the problem—Harvey's and hers, for all families were the same—in a focus as clear as a Renaissance portrait. "Don't try to make up for past errors. Assume you did the best you could at the time and let them decide whether to accept you now or not."

"You're very wise," Harvey Porter said.

"Talk is cheap," said Beverly.

They agreed to spend one last day and then part forever. They made two more deceitful phone calls. After a Hot Shoppe breakfast, they started to walk toward the Capitol. They would spend this last day together and then they would take different night planes home. As they liked it. No complications. Beverly belonged to her family. Harvey's wife needed him. There was no question of hanging on. They stood on a high corner of New Jersey Avenue, looking across at the dome. "It's a beautiful building," Beverly admitted. She admired its dignity, the serenity of its proportions.

"We don't have to go inside," Harvey Porter said. "As long as we know it's there."

CHAPTER 8 _____

He wanted a robe.

"What for? We're going home today."

"Not until tonight. I'll have a good part of the afternoon to wear the robe for you."

"I have no objection to naked."

He had always wanted a libertine robe. Something sensual and satanic, black silk with a dragon on the back. He had never indulged himself. Now he thought he should have it. He punched the air. He *would* have it.

They floated, like two hydrofoils adrift, so little above the surface of the busy sidewalks that nobody not looking hard could see that their feet—her wide Picasso feet in oxfords and his narrow Degas feet in shined black moccasins—were not quite touching ground. Corners they took in little airborne swoops, but what with the heavy midmorning traffic, nobody noticed that either. Afloat beside him, trailing in some story of his about a hike along the Appalachian Trail, remembering how much she had talked yesterday and how speechless she was today, a post-coital listener, struck dumb, passivated by passion, transformed into the real female receptacle, The Ear, perfectly content that way, too, she walked, listened, and steered him through the downtown streets to the improbably fashionable front of Garwood's, where she knew he would find a really patrician dressing gown, redolent of Old Newport as she imagined it.

A back-bent mannequin in the window, clearly an orthopedic case, wore a sack of a black dress. "I know where she's going in that black dress," Harvey said. "She's going to a meeting of the Vanishing Species Society. She's chairman of the Save the Tiger Ball. She will have her photograph taken for the social page of the Washington *Post*. She'll be seated, no doubt, on a leopard-skin sofa."

How mild he is, Beverly suddenly thought, *in relation to the intensity of his feelings. How fierce I am in relation to the shallowness of mine.* And at the same time, in another key, she was thinking that the black dress was very nice but too short-sleeved for her chunky arms.

They moved on toward the entrance where forty-dollar-an-ounce perfume rolled out the revolving door and gathered them up and floated them in—the two of them in one section, a bit of a squeeze—and set them aglide over the marble floors among the polished and laden counters where Harvey failed to see his fellow shoppers as individuals with trouble or kindness in their eyes and Beverly forgot to shed disdain on all the hard women with their husband's money on their back or rage at the greedy array of offensive luxury—gloves on flower stems, handbags on easels, jewelry on Fontainebleau busts, blouses laid out like Violetta's death scene. Harvey, though, was unable to cross the first floor, even on his love-propelled conveyor belt, without eying a pouchy leather handbag he wished he could send to his daughter Kitty, thinking about a paisley blouse for Suzy, and then, a little guiltily, catching sight of a pair of driving gloves that Sally might like.

Beverly, the erstwhile wonderful mother, walked through the merchandise as if it were dust. She was thinking about Harvey's robe.

Connecting smoothly, they glided up the escalator to the men's-wear shop on the second floor, where the robes looked like dressing gowns for conservative congressmen. Beverly thought any one would be perfect. Harvey disagreed. "I need a robe to have an affair in," he told the salesman, an elderly Aryan, who nodded soberly and directed them upstairs to the "Unisex Bizarre."

Four flights up was more to Harvey's liking. The "Unisex Bizarre" was a discreet mauve corner boxed on a floor of small specialty shops and was designed to spare its occupants the awkwardness of direct communication. A juke box was making a lot of noise and sharp, insolently colored lights were flashing. Distortion and obfuscation were carried out in the merchandise, for the racks were stuffed with clothing that looked more like hardware or forest animals or weapons. Furthermore, there was no way to discern which garment was to cover what part of the human body. Back was front, up was down, waistline was hip, neckband was leghole. Beverly didn't like the place. Harvey was delighted with it.

Beverly pushed into the racks and managed to wrest out an apple-green chambray robe, floor length, that looked to her like summer in Newport.

"Too *goyish*," Harvey Porter said. "Not enough dash."

He chose for himself a sinister, medieval-looking garment, a long, skinny cassock with a mandarin collar and in heavy black silk. He handed Beverly his suit coat and slipped into the Tangier special. In Harvey's head, a dragon on the back licked its smoking tongue at Beverly as Harvey turned modestly away to tie the sash. Harvey was fat around the middle and the tassled ends of the sash hung shorter, less brazenly than intended. "I'm afraid," he said, disappointed, "that without more overlap this sash fails to serve its primary purpose."

"What's that? I never read de Sade."

"To keep the robe closed, it seems to me."

"Oh, yes. Well, try this one." She held out the apple-green chambray. "You'll wear it in Waddingford and nobody will even guess that you played around in Washington."

"Yes. That's why I don't want it."

He was busy in the racks and fished out a knee-length sheer acetate with wide sleeves and naked orange lions disporting themselves in fields of cornflower blue. Harvey looked for a dressing room so he could take off his pants. He told Beverly that length in the boudoir was very important; the shape of a leg much affected by the placement of the hemline. He disappeared with the kingly beasts over his arm and soon returned from a distant dressing room. Beverly stood watching. There was no leg in sight. The tall man's robe reached the short man's sock tops. "You are ridiculous," she said. "Who could get a hard on with you running around in a circus tent?"

At last Beverly found what she was looking for. Mashed between sequined pajamas and a blouse that seemed to be made of cellophane, she found a robe that moved her. She tugged it out. It was a deep red velours robe—plain, capacious, and soft. It was a robe that looked both sensuous and serious, sending a scent of sex up her nose and a tantalizing twitch up her bottom front. Without remembering why, Beverly badly wanted that velvety, winy robe on Harvey on her.

The red velours was right. Even over trousers. "I am impressed with its warmth," Harvey said, looking kingly and monkish in it, looking young and blooded and ready. "As for its aesthetic qualities, I feel incapable of judging it other than to say it is silky smooth and flowing."

"Madman!" Beverly went into her handbag and came out with a checkbook. "I know it's a little low key for your taste," she said. "But I want you to do me a favor and take it anyway."

A unisex salesperson appeared like a rocket at sight of the checkbook.

Harvey looked at the tag on the red velours pocket.

"Forty-five dollars!" he exploded. "For a bathrobe? You could dress a whole Indian village for that money!"

"Yes, but you can't," Beverly soothed him. "I know those mathematics from leftovers at my dinner table." She began writing the check. "Take the robe and when you get home you can send a contribution to CARE."

Harvey was fighting his way under the red velours and into his pants pocket. "I'm paying," he said. He drew out his wallet like a dueling pistol.

"No. I'm paying. It's my gift."

"You make me want to shout at you."

"Look. You'd never buy a fifty-dollar robe for yourself."

"Except on this occasion, when I want to. And it's forty-five."

Harvey fumbled wrathfully with bills and travelers' checks. Beverly pressed her advantage and the salesperson took her check and driver's license. Harvey's face began to approach the color of the robe. "Shall I have it wrapped," she asked him, "or are you going to wear it?"

Harvey stared at her. She saw how deeply she had probed beneath his mild manners. Beneath his gentility.

"*Macho*," she said.

The reply *Bitch* formed on his lips. But they were Puritan lips as well as macho lips and so he made no sound.

Not much later, when Harvey sufferingly admitted that he had felt for a moment *really* angry at her, Beverly could hardly believe how deeply it troubled him. Ashamed of wanting to hit somebody over the head? What nonsense! As long as you didn't hit. Furthermore, Harvey Porter needn't feel he was so special as to be above reacting negatively to a woman's man-to-man defiance. A lot of otherwise civilized men reacted negatively. Got mad. Wanted to hit, punch, curse, or even cripple a woman who forgot to know her place. "Stop torturing yourself," Beverly told him. "It's natural to get mad.

"Here you were brought up to be such a gentleman and what happens? You do the right thing and it's gone out of style."

Time was when Beverly *liked* men to open doors for her. She *enjoyed* having her dinner paid for. The nicest part of being a woman (aside from the prospect of bearing one's own children) was the courtliness of men—which could be encouraged by gracious behavior.

The winds of change had blown in one gusty March day with her old college friend Mollie Parish. Beverly was leaving Saks Fifth Avenue, loaded down with spring clothes for Allison, and the strong wind literally blew her into Mollie, who was standing on the Fiftieth Street corner taking an orgasm survey. "Excuse me," Mollie said when they collided. It was both an apology and an introduction. "Excuse me, but would you possibly be able to answer just a few questions on this survey for *Continental* magazine?"

Beverly hated *Continental* magazine for its simpering copy and the half-naked women on its cover—why did they use sneaky Boy Scout sex appeal to attract women readers? who looks like that naked anyway?—so she meant to refuse. But it was her habit to look at people even when refusing them, and a close look showed up Mollie Parish with her stringy hair pulled into a bun and the figure that had been ample in "new look" skirts and ruffled blouses still ample in a linty black suit cut short above the knees of snagged stockings. The heart-shaped face was as good-natured as ever. They hadn't met for fifteen years and Beverly was stirred. "Mollie! What are you doing here?"

"I'm taking this godawful survey," she said as if they came together every day. She rattled the papers. She had an old-lady handbag over one arm and an extra pencil behind her ear. "None of these women will answer my questions. I've been using my friends but my friends aren't exactly typical. The magazine wants real people. Are you a real person, Beverly?"

Beverly looked at a page of questions.

HOW OFTEN DO YOU ENGAGE IN SEXUAL INTERCOURSE?

daily   3 times a week   twice a week
weekly   twice monthly   other

HOW OFTEN DO YOU ATTAIN ORGASM?

always   sometimes   never
frequently   seldom   other

HOW OFTEN DO YOU MASTURBATE?

The survey wanted specifics such as present age, age at menarche, first copulation, first orgasm, number of lovers before, during, and after marriage, preferences regarding style of sexual intercourse, and number of participants. Beverly thought it was a wonder her friend hadn't been arrested.

"Take some surveys home with you," Mollie begged. "Take some for your neighbors. I'd really appreciate it." She ran after another prospect, a woman in a sari, a group of fur-coated shoppers, an elderly nun. Nobody would take her survey. "We're trying to de-mythify the vaginal orgasm," she called to Beverly.

A pair of men in suits with vests stopped, looked, and went on again. Beverly stuffed the papers into her shopping bag. "Some people are coming up Friday night," Mollie said. "Some women from the movement. Why don't you join us?"

"Where?"

"At my place." Mollie said it as if it were self-evident. And added with an understanding smile, "Husbands are invited."

There was a lineup at the elevator in the fashionable

lobby of Mollie Parish's apartment building, a New York spread of people inured to being in crowds, crowded. The elevator arrived, took in a load of them, and left a big crowd still waiting. It was not, Beverly could tell at a glance, going to be a Saturday night with the people next door.

She well remembered the arrogant city parties Peter used to take her to when he was starting out in business. Young Peter with his soul in his smile—an arrow shot into the air by a family of expectant Jews—advanced from group to group of cannon-chested, boulder-shouldered bull-backed businessmen while Beverly—dressed to be well-dressed, comporting herself to be a credit to her husband and her parents, too, in case anybody knew them—sat sunk in a chair at the wives' table talking about babies and recipes (furniture might be construed as show-offy and she was still too young for Paris restaurants and Caribbean beaches). The present party would be different, Beverly expected.

The elevator returned and the crowd plunged in, Peter pulling Beverly against him before the gate closed. Wedged into Beverly was a small, dark woman with a baby—about two months old, Beverly estimated—strapped to her chest. Beverly asked if she was a friend of Mollie's.

The small woman shook her head. "The Voice said there was going to be a party here, so I came."

Peg Booker, a Big Mommy of the feminist movement, was up front. Beverly recognized her from news pictures, a small chesty woman, who looked like a bargain hunter in a very low-cut dress. Adam Lasher was flattened against the elevator wall. His photograph ran beside his articles in Gotham Weekly, but Beverly would have guessed that he was a reporter because he had the busiest eyes she had ever seen—eyes that watched the door, studied the crowd, listened and sniffed and surely could see around corners to pounce on evidence (real, circumstantial, manufactured) for a magazine that specialized in quick gratification of all sorts of appetites—never mind the heartburn.

In one corner was a very old, white-haired woman who, someone whispered, had written a health book. Jammed against the gate was a not-so-old bald man who, somebody else said, was the most powerful agent in the Queens County prosecutor's office. Four roseate middle-aged men, tailored and coiffed to a high shine, had evidently come from a cocktail party. There was a white woman all dressed in leather and a black woman all dressed in white and young girls in boots and old men in denims and couples and threesomes, singles and amorphous groupings, and when the elevator at last reached the eleventh-floor landing, they all surged forth only to splash against an oncoming wave of departing guests. Only Peg Booker, like a prow, forced herself against the tide and, bared bosom first, penetrated the party. The rest went down again, pressed even tighter than before, and had to wait for two or three more downcoming loads before they could break into the apartment. Peter wanted to leave even before he learned he had to pay to get in.

"Per couple is cool," the young woman at the cashbox said. She sat at a card table between the vestibule and the living room. "It was ten dollars apiece before," she explained, "but now there isn't any food left." Beside the cashbox was a photograph of a little house with white shingles and ivy. WOMEN'S HISTORY LIBRARY AND RESEARCH CENTER was printed on the mounting. Peter forked up the money but Beverly avoided his eyes. The cashier pointed to the room where the bar was, down a hall about as crowded as the elevator.

It was a big party. In a back bedroom the small woman nursed her baby on top of a pile of coats on a bed where two other women were sitting and arguing about women's rights in South Africa. In a child's room, an author in a jumpsuit was swinging at a book reviewer in a toupee and shrieking at him, "Sexist bastard!" while the rest of the people watched with benign interest. There was no telling what was going on in the bedroom that had been made a bar, though Peter tried to edge his way through the thick of it. The living room was impassable, people bunched as tight as asparagus from the stained-glass screen to the fishnet wall and piled on couches like the coats in the bedroom. "I'm planning my life with a flow chart," one guest said. "It was more interesting before."

Through it all wove Mollie Parish in a kind of white floating pantsuit with low-hanging sleeves and a button missing. Mollie, towing Karen X., a chunky post-deb with a truculent face and eyes that went vacant when she was asked about the Women's History Library and Research Center, which she was building in two rooms of her house near Bloomington, Indiana. Mollie introduced her as a saint.

Dim as Beverly's perceptions were at this crowded time of her life, she saw that Mollie's party was no ordinary event. The glitter and clout were not imaginary. The women were movers. Of course, Beverly did not want to be like them, but still she was glad to see there was no wives' table. She looked out from under her fat, her docility, her pleasantness, and saw women, energized and intense, pushing through, holding forth, coming across, breaking out. They were not using their energy to wipe down refrigerators, these women. They were not using their intensity to badger their kids. A woman in a flowered kimono and flowers in her waist-length hair sailed by and was identified as Jessica Faber. Even Beverly recognized the name of the feminist sociologist. Beryl Kasner, the feminist psychologist, was there, too, dark as a mole, in a man's suit with vest and ascot, smoking a cigarillo. Against the dining-room table, which was spread with scraped-empty trays, cheese rinds, a few bread crusts, and bitten-into pickles, three taut young women argued about the merits of street demonstrations while a noted woman wrestler forced her way into the kitchen and found piles of trays of unserved food. As guests invaded the kitchen, Pamela McCaffery, the distinguished literary critic who looked and sounded like an old-fashioned schoolmarm, told Beverly that the vagina is a more subtle and finished organ than the penis and Chloris Bevan, the Boston pacifist, told Pamela McCaffery and Beverly that womb envy was the root of all evil. Jessica Faber told everyone that she had never been so happy with her husband of twenty years as she now was with her female lover, who was not on a domination trip.

At least two women called Beverly *Sister*. A man, somebody's husband, wistfully asked her what *she* did. Wistfully she told him, "I take care of my husband and children." The man—he had a frankfurter face: long nose, long chin, baggy eyes—said he was in the garment line and wanted to tell Beverly a joke about an elephant he had met in a downtown bar. Beverly excused herself.

Had she ever done such a thing before?

No. Never before had she been able to pump out of herself the courage to avoid being bored.

Had she ever been bored?

She didn't know. Now she knew she didn't want to hear this man tell a joke.

She preferred to be among the women. The women were—how unusual! how unprecedented!—more interesting.

Homeward, in the car, she shimmered. She felt like a pinball machine, with running blood and a lit-up head. She couldn't stop talking about the party.

"You know, Peter, if Jessica Faber were a man I wouldn't think she was so crazy. A man can get lost in the middle of a sentence and we say he's an absent-minded professor. He can wear silly clothes or flirt with young girls or be terribly finicky about his food. Whatever a man does, it's okay. It's maybe a little eccentric, but we don't make a big case of it or question his competence on the job. But let a woman act a bit nutty, right away she's a crazy lady and nothing she does is taken seriously. We're all so intolerant of . . ."

Peter turned on the radio news.

Some of Beverly's lights went out, but she didn't care. It was midnight: she was glad he had let her stay so late. She pulled into a corner of the seat and curled up with her thoughts. The women took over. The loud and the rude, the cold, scowling, overbearing, and interrupting horde of unlikable, unendearing females danced in her head. They would probably not even offer you coffee if you came to their house. They would let a child out in cold weather without a sweater. But those women were not lost under their clothes or swallowed up by their smiles. And Beverly decided she wouldn't mind getting her own cup of coffee.

On the other hand, like all tough women, they made her nervous. These friends of Mollie's would not hesitate to upset

a person. You'd have to be careful what you asked them because they would not hesitate to give you an answer. She
wondered what Peter thought about the party, but she knew
he would not give her the answer. He was listening to the
weather report.

It was not until months after the Bar Mitzvah that Beverly
heard again from Mollie Parish. By that time Beverly was thick
with gloom and apprehension and she heard the phone like
the tolling of iron bells. Mollie on the other end was as breezy
as if she called every day. She talked about great occasions as if
Beverly had been there. She talked about famous people as if
Beverly knew them. Somewhere in the onrushing tide of talk,
she insisted that Beverly come to a Women's Rights Conference on the next Saturday. Mollie was to be a speaker. Beverly
had to be there. Beverly was so numb that she went.

"Older women are the garbage of our society!"
The little woman on the podium was not old but she
looked prematurely desiccated. She seemed to need the support of the microphone stand. Her voice quavered and yet,
altogether, she packed a wallop. The women in the audience
stood up and cheered.

The school auditorium was filled beyond capacity. Women
sat on window sills, on the floor between the aisles, stood in
the doorway and against the walls. Beverly had arrived early
and taken a seat up front where she could be reassured by the
occasional attention of Mollie up at the table on the platform.
Knowing Mollie was there, having been personally greeted,
she felt a little more entitled to be present though she could
not quite break out of the semi-transparent envelope that
seemed to separate her from the bona fide audience. They

were a great variety of women. Beverly could see herself
among them—the overweight, docile, good Jewish girls who
telephoned their mother every day. And she could see her
mother there, too, the sharp Sadie Pecks who took care of
everything, wearing their fierce mask of judgment. Depressed
though she was, Beverly saw that these familiars sat comfortably among more exotic species—crazily dressed women, tough
women, intellectuals, Latins, Anglo-Saxons, very old women,
college women, businesswomen, who thumped the floor and
cheered when the birdy woman at the microphone repeated,
this time in a near hysterical pitch: "That's how our society
deals with older women. Like garbage!"

Beverly thought of Sadie—cleaning her house intermina-
bly, cooking for two in pots big enough for ten in the hope that
somebody might drop in and eat something. Bringing food to
Beverly's house and sniffing with disappointment if nobody
gobbled it up. Packing small activities into oversized days.
Playing cards. Shopping for things she didn't need. Answering
the cheerful *How're you doing?* with a plaintive *I keep myself
busy.* On Saturdays when Ben was in the store, riding out to
Heightsville on the "mothers" bus—a sad bus, a busful of
women, husbandless grandmothers, coming to spend a day of
temporary inclusion with their children's families. And on
other days, Sadie waited. Waited for phone calls. For visits.
For a game program to come up on television. For something
to happen, for someone to need her, for Ben to come home
and eat what she had cooked for him. What Sadie would do
without Ben, Beverly could not permit herself to imagine.
Beverly sat feeling cold and bloodless. What Beverly would
ever do without her family to live for, she could not think
about either.

The sharp, sere little woman on the podium was ranting

about the "Mother's Day package," which she called "the world's greatest hype." Beverly drew her sweater tightly around her and sank deeper into her chair. What silly women these women were, she thought. Battling against Mother's Day. A bunch of malcontents, she thought. Oddballs. What were all these women doing here on a Saturday? Who was taking care of their children? Now they were applauding the speech. As if they'd blow up the room. Beverly wondered who was crazy, she or they?

Next up was a woman as fierce as a totem pole. A lawyer from the Coast with sequins in her afro hairdo and heavy earrings that hung to her shoulders. She had a man-eating figure, in tailored pants and a glamorous sweater, and her fingernails were like jungle claws. When she had stamped out the cheering, she started to send fire through her eyes and her shouting mouth.

"They tell us who we are and what we're good for," she roared. "And we are for their convenience."

The roil was inside her. "They say we're helpless and they won't give us help." She stared straight at Beverly. "You try getting a bank loan. Try to get a credit card on your name. Try to get a mortgage when your husband leaves you."

Beverly knew nothing about mortgages. She wouldn't even know where to go. This wild black woman was out of her world.

"They say we need protection so they sit on us to keep us needing protection." She left the microphone and came out among the audience: "Honey," she addressed a tame-looking blonde. "Next time some nice gentleman wants to hold open a door for you, you tell him screw the door, you want a chance to learn his job and earn his paycheck, so you don't have to depend on somebody like him to be kind enough to take care of you when you aren't blonde and pretty any more."

"Sweetheart," she told a plump matron, "next time a nice man offers you his seat on a bus, tell him to keep his seat and get you a promotion on your job, so you don't have to be content at fifty years old to stand behind a counter for two dollars an hour on your feet all day selling shit to shit-eaters!"

She was back at her microphone, all on fire now. "You know what happens if your husband beats you up and blacks your eye and opens your head?

"Judge tells you kiss and make up, go on home and stop that bickering.

"You know what happens if your husband does that same violence to another man?"

"Atrocious assault!" the audience yelled. And yelled some more.

"Damn right!" the speaker yelled back at them.

Mollie Parish, set to speak next, didn't see Beverly looking at her. Mollie was listening to Fran Bodgins, laying it down. And Mollie was weeping. Beverly was astonished to see, from twenty feet away, quiet swells of tears filling and flowing from Mollie's soft eyes.

Between speeches there was a demonstration in the audience. A group of women, filling most of two or three rows, moved to eject four men—a television camera crew, who had been working up front and staying out of the way when they weren't working. The band of women stood up and shouted: "No men wanted! No men wanted!" They were a tough-looking, clench-fisted lot. One shouted, "Send in a women's crew!" and the shout was taken up. The TV men were caught unprepared. They looked toward the conference leaders. The program was stopped; the women continued to shout. Other women joined the protest. The leaders met, and finally someone asked the camera crew to leave. Most of the audience cheered as the workingmen quietly, resignedly rolled up their wires, folded their light stands, hauled up the lights and cameras, making a slow dance of it all, and at last pulled out. Beverly didn't cheer. She was embarrassed by the behavior of the other women. (*Like the uppity Jews?* she wondered at herself. *The decorous Jews who are ashamed of the table of loud Jews near them in the restaurant?*) Aloud she said, "The poor guys are only trying to make a living." The woman beside her agreed. "But don't you think," the woman, Beverly's age but in fighting trim, reasonably added, "that the TV station might have sent a camera crew of women?" Beverly thought she'd think about it . . .

"You may find this a little bit lunatic fringy," Mollie warned her. "Don't come if you don't want to. You could go to Banking and Finance. Or Divorce Law or Alternate Life Styles."

The Know Your Body workshop did not much appeal to Beverly, though Mollie needed to go for background in her survey work. Actually Banking and Finance didn't interest her either; Beverly was very bad with money and was glad Peter handled all the bills and investments. Divorce Law interested her not at all, thank God. But Alternate Life Styles—there was something. Beverly occasionally dreamed of living differently. Alone in a Paris flat for example. Reading and taking long walks. Beverly found the classroom where the Alternate Life

Styles workshop was being conducted. Inside, seated at and on the desks, were the members of the burly, militant contingent that had got rid of the cameramen. They were the Radical Feminists, whose idea of an alternate life style was not running away to Paris, but simply eliminating men, cropping them out of the picture, erasing them, pushing them off the road. The women were direct, sharp. Beverly liked the way they got to the point. An all-woman commune. An all-woman apartment building. These women who had only recently picketed a bar that did not allow women were discussing the possibility of opening a For Women Only bar and restaurant.

Beverly listened to make sure she was hearing it right. Convinced that nobody was going to mention a pied-à-terre in Paris, she slipped out to find Mollie at the Know Your Body class.

Having always shut her eyes during the delicate part of gynecological examinations, Beverly had never actually seen a speculum. Therefore, she was unprepared—upon opening the door of Room 214—for the sight of a woman lying on her back over two children's worktables with her skirt up around her waist, her legs pulled up, her knees spread wide, and a line of women waiting their turn to look up a plastic tube that was inserted in her vagina.

Even if she had seen a speculum before, Beverly might have been taken aback by the procedures of the Know Your Body workshop.

Mollie Parish provided no comfort. "We have never been allowed to see or understand the workings of our own bodies," Mollie explained when Beverly clutched her arm. "These women," Mollie explained, "go all over the country teaching self-examination." As Mollie spoke, another young woman had clambered onto another pair of tables and taken the position. It was a very well-attended workshop and the line of women, very serious and very enthusiastic, moved along, each woman peering earnestly into the first plastic speculum, then going to the end of the next line.

"Did you ever see a cervix?" Mollie pulled Beverly into line.

Beverly Gordon had never been averse to the element of mystery in life, but her curiosity had always been tempered by a strong sense of self-preservation. She wished there were a less bizarre way to penetrate these organic mysteries. However, when she found herself in the front of the line, she bent down and peered through the speculum and made acquaintance with the cervix of the young, very pink-faced woman who was lying on the two tables and talking all the time, apparently overjoyed with the experience of making her private parts public. What she was talking about while Beverly looked up her was the hygienic necessity of a speculum in every boudoir and monthly (if not more frequent) self-examinations. "Do it with your Sisters, with your CR group," she breezily admonished her audience. "You can all get together and familiarize yourselves with your bodies."

Beverly looked in the speculum and saw a smooth white plane with a red spot in the middle. "There's a big red spot on your cervix," she told Exhibit A.

"I know," the young woman replied. "It's just an irritation. From the speculum."

"Did everybody get a look?" Exhibit B called from behind her tent of skirt. She was as excited as Exhibit A and didn't want Beverly to pass her by. "As soon as everybody's finished with my cervix," she said, "you're going to take turns looking at each other's."

"I've really got to get home," Beverly told Mollie, who decided she could also do without the next item on the agenda, a demonstration of the new suction method for extracting the menstrual flow all at once. Putting a period on periods, they called it in California. Mollie already knew about it. She was preparing a survey of medical opinion on the subject. Mollie and Beverly slipped out together.

This was not like dessert with the Temple Sisterhood, all the ladies getting fat together on homemade ladyfinger mousse cake and brandy-soaked syllabub. Here, at the Consciousness-Raising group, there was a businesslike coffeepot and seven mugs. No candy basket. No new ensembles from Claire and May's discount boutique on the Old Highway Route. They were seven women who had been thinking about other things while they were dressing. Seven women in the living room of a modest Burntwood house, telling one another why they were there.

Ruth, over fifty, is a flimsily built woman with a narrow, sad face and wheat-colored hair in a ponytail. She has never worked at a regular job because she wants to be free to accompany her husband on vacations and business trips whenever opportunities arise. She is not dissatisfied. Why did she join a Consciousness-Raising group? She doesn't know. She suffers from unease. She is afraid to go out alone. She has felt a bit random since her only daughter married and went to live in Canada. She is not unhappy, just uncertain, but very proud to be part of this group.

Gert knows why she is here. She has got to get some

support from her Sisters. Gert is under thirty. Her flat, sure face is squarely framed with black bangs and straight-hanging hair. Her baby is four months old and very seductive, Gert says. If Gert chooses to stay home with the baby, her husband will be happy to provide for all of them. Gert is tempted by the offer. She has extended her leave from the brokerage firm at which she is a junior partner. But she knows they won't hold her place forever.

Sylvia, in her forties, has red hair and a kind, bumpy face. She works in a beauty parlor. Her husband comes home from his work tired and wants to watch TV. With Sylvia beside him. He also wants hot meals, a spotless house, and everything his way. Sylvia says, to hell with him. This is my life, too. If I want to go out bowling, I go. That's because I get confidence from my CR group. Last year I stayed home all the time.

Vera is fat and dramatic and in her late thirties. Her graying dark hair falls in torrents around a face that is swollen with self-pity. "Anything I want from life I have to get for myself," she cries. "I must support myself and my children because my husband is dysfunctional. I must battle the institutions of this world which are run by men for men." Every week some man does Vera wrong. Promises to buy a dozen, then buys only four. Keeps her waiting. Breaks an appointment. "Men," Vera complains, "are unable to deal with a truly independent woman, so they always fuck her over."

Bunny is sharp-faced and tense, almost thirty-five and married to a man no longer interested in her, maybe turned off on sex in general. Who knows? Bunny shrugs. "Who can talk to a man when he's like that? A month goes by with him, and nothing." Bunny has kinky hair the color of ginger ale and there is a fizzy quality in her very sexy blue eyes. She has been looking for new interests now that her children are all in school. She has been looking around for a job and, in the looking, she sometimes meets interesting men. Bunny wants to know what the other women think—do—about outside lovers.

Joan left her husband two years ago when she was forty. He had become impossible to live with. He hated his job; he was angry at the world. He took his frustrations out on Joan and the boys. She got a job to help him make a new start, but it didn't work out. Home life worsened. Joan, both righteous and full of guilt, left him and took an apartment with the boys. She fell into a panic, took a young lover, continued to panic, worried about her husband, could neither eat nor sleep, felt apprehension boring like a gorge that would split her in two. The lover turned out to be too young, too shallow, too irresponsible. Her husband became valuable in comparison. Joan hated the young singles set—pressure-cooker people, she called them. She went back to her husband, who took revenge by not taking revenge, never berating her, asking no questions, hiding his hurt. Joan is a woman with great intensity behind her gentle, plain, appealing, frightened face. No one from the CR group telephones her home, for Joan's husband would surely feel threatened if he learned of her connection to the Movement.

Beverly, almost forty, suspects that she is cheating the group. She has no problems, really. She has a good husband and good children. The kids are at that exciting age when every day brings something new—their school, their friends, never a dull moment. Her husband lets her do anything she wants. She has adjusted to her role, which is—who would deny it?—an important one: to make a home for a family, bring up decent future citizens. Beverly's house is a haven for her husband, a hangout for her children and their friends. Beverly keeps busy, helping out at the children's schools, at her Temple. She nevers says No when a charity calls and asks her to collect on her block. She bakes for bake sales. She volunteers. Beverly is one of the angels of this earth—not the wispy heavenly type, but the muscular kind of angel who holds things together, the puttying angel who fills up all the holes and seals the cracks.

Why should she think of changing her calling? Why should a house cat dream of becoming a lion? Who would trade tranquil hours in the garden, the gracious writing table or tea cart (not that Beverly lived that way, but she could, she *could*), for an intense, anxious, unfamiliar, and lonely road into an unpredictable future? Beverly was one of the luckiest of women. She didn't have to get up in the morning. Why should she think of business hours, rushing to appointments, *having* to get dressed, competition, wrangling, tension, the heart attacks and other headaches that might easily be left to the men?

Especially if she didn't need the money?

Beverly has no real problem, but she has been depressed lately. A little bit lost. A little bit helpless. A little bit too dependent upon other people to make her feel useful. A little bit overly needful of reassurance from the husband she married right out of her parents' overly protective house. Frankly, she is secretly afraid to displease him because she is even more secretly afraid he will leave her. So she bends herself to make him dependent upon her. Call it love that she cooks what he likes to eat, that she goes where he points to, that she offers him unquestioning comfort and support. But secretly she is so dependent that she doesn't know whether she loves him or not. Recently she noticed how her voice rises when she is talking to Peter. She has been hearing herself turn into a little girl in Peter's company. One day she turned from a phone call with Mollie Parish to talk to Peter, and her voice slid up, up and she heard with dismay the voice of a little girl of almost thirty-nine. What kind of wife was that? What kind of woman was that?

Sometimes Peter complains that she hangs on him too much. This is treason. She always kept herself down so that he could stand high. He used to stand on the step stool of her helplessness and now he complains that she leans too heavily on him. Call the plumber herself. Order theater subscriptions without him: he never liked Shakespeare. Figure her own bank balance. Other women lead their own lives. Yet he is kindest to her when she is most helpless. Peter is forty and he says he feels encumbered. He married too young. He should have lived more. Beverly is afraid.

But she has nothing to say at her CR group. The other women speak their woes, put shape to their doubts. Beverly, who is better adjusted, listens to them and is hardly aware of the small empty space where the pit would be if she were a prune.

The Trojan Women, she secretly describes them, with their talk about love and scorn, pity and fear; the need to please and the need to nourish; the desire for approval; the longing for a great passion; the urge to achieve and the fear of competition; mother as conscience, father as lover; the shame of wanting more than is offered, the outrage of getting less than is fair. Beverly was moved by and envious of their intelli-

gence and intensity. They met on Thursday afternoons at
three o'clock and talked until it was after five and time to hurry
home to make dinner.

"I love you," Joan said to Vera, "but you are talking
bullshit.

"Seems to me you are taking a long self-pity trip. Don't
you think businessmen have the same problems as businesswomen? Seems I've heard men complain about being kept
waiting and being stood up. I think it's a people problem more
than a woman problem.

"I also wonder," Joan said, getting up and crossing to
Vera's chair, "if when a person starts believing that the whole
world is out to get her, maybe she's asking for it." She kissed
Vera on the cheek and Vera smiled up ruefully at her, nodding
thanks.

"But Ruth," Gert pondered. "Don't you feel restless just
waiting around till your husband decides what he wants to do?
Don't you feel nonexistent?"

"I do some volunteer work," Ruth explained. "It keeps me
busy, but it sometimes makes me fretful when a temporary is
called in and paid for what I do free. The paid worker is always
treated with more respect than I get. People assume I have
nothing better to do and I guess they're right."

"My husband and I went on a cruise," Bunny said. "After
a week of me coming on in my sexy cruise wear and him taking
walks on the deck all night, I got disgusted. I mean, how much
rejection can you take? So on the eighth day, I smiled back at
the cabin boy. It was the Greek line. For the last four days of
that cruise I really lived. He was twenty-four, very beautiful,

very strong, very grateful, and he could hardly talk English, which made it even better."

"Didn't you feel guilty?" Joan and Ruth asked, almost at once.

"No," Bunny told them. "I felt proud. I was proud to be enough of a grownup to know what I needed and to go after it."

"Did your husband get suspicious?" Sylvia wanted to know.

"I told him after the first time. Actually the first time was four times altogether—you know these Mediterraneans. Then when I told my husband, he got aroused finally. I don't know, he got very excited. The last three days were with my husband."

"My husband wanted me to be the woman his mother was. Like, have eight children and cook soup. I used to feel very inadequate that four children were a handful for me," Vera said, musingly.

"I bet now he wishes his mother was the woman you are so she could support herself."

Beverly loved these women who trusted one another and who learned from their trust that they were not alone, not weird, not unnatural in their feelings. Beverly loved their good sense, their vulnerability, their determination to make better lives for themselves. Any one of these women might have sat with her, in the old days, at the wives' table. The blood and fire was always there, compressed and secured in the old days, while the women exchanged recipes and tight smiles. Everybody had blood and fire, Beverly knew now. Even she herself.

Beverly was throwing her weight around. Old Paint; Shlepalong, Peter used to call her. She was like a teddy bear but now his pet names didn't go. He pulled her hat over her eyes one day, friendly gesture, and she gave him hell.

After all he'd done. Look at the house they lived in. Four bathrooms. The best stove money could buy, plus a wall oven. He had spared nothing. She wanted a built-in dressing table; he surprised her for her birthday. She wanted central air conditioning; no questions asked. Parties. Gardeners. Peter had done all this for a poor girl from the Bronx and now, all of a sudden, the things he had done were no longer valuable to her. She didn't want to cook. She didn't want to get dressed up. Now she wanted to go to school and hang around with a bunch of grubby kids, pot smokers, dropouts, welfare cheats. She wanted to go to women's lib meetings and talk about her sex life. All right, Peter had said to himself, times change. If this is what she wants, let her have it. But he would not compromise himself. He would not sit in his living room with his wife's friends who were young enough to be her children and if they were her children she would have asked them to take a shower and put on some clean clothes and get a paying job, damn it. He would not put up with his son Sandy carrying on like these guys, and he, Peter, would not pussyfoot among them, pretending to approve of spongers and drifters who did not pay their dues no matter how much they pretended to know about fourteenth-century madonnas and twentieth-century perversions, and he was also not going to take any putdowns and ballbreakings from her women's lib friends, either.

It was burdensome, all this flak, back talk, not knowing what would come next. He felt her weight on him. She inter-

fered with his business. *Did you pay the hardware store bill,*
she said. *Please pay it or let me make a check. I'm embarrassed*
to go in there. That was not her business. Furthermore, she
found fault with the way he talked to his children. She was
getting so fat, Beverly. It disgusted him.

In Washington Beverly had met a man who liked her. He
did not mind her exuberance or her experimental independence. But he did not want her to pay for his robe.

Piecing together the scraps of information she had
gathered—the car he drove, the places he went, the cut of his
suit, the sheen of his shirts, the length of time it took him to
decide to call a taxi, the depth of attention he gave to figuring
out a tip—Beverly concluded that Harvey Porter was not
rolling in money, and she did not want him to feel sad or guilty
over the extravagance of the robe.

But on the other hand, she saw that he did not want her to
pay. So, smiling in defeat, she called the salesperson and took
back her check. Harvey paid cash and got the box, which he
swung in its gold shopping bag.

"Your place or my place?" he asked on the down escalator.

"My place," Beverly said.

CHAPTER 9

"Is there someplace you'd like to go first?"

He is not in his twenties, Beverly bethought herself. *Older men have trouble. For God's sake, even Peter has trouble once in a while.*

"I don't want to insult you," she said. "But I'd really like to see the Impressionists at the National Gallery. And then we could go back if you want to."

He was sure she meant it. He hoped she did. He would hate to disappoint her. He could not bear for her to think he did not find her attractive.

"Really, Harvey. I just like *being* with you. It could be anyplace as long as we're close. But maybe best in a museum."

185

"One of the compensations of aging," he said, "might be the ability to dispense one's energies with budgetary considerations. Coosting in a corner, so to speak."

They walked toward the Mall. She took his hand. "You know, you are very beautiful," he said with a shade of wonder because he had not thought so the day before.

Complexity. A comeuppance was not undeserved, Harvey Porter thought. Adultery had not been uncommitted. The excitement of the novelty had swept him into undiluted passion. Anxiety had been overwhelmed. But the morning's reflection had opened the gate and whistled it back.

They crossed over the new subway line, circling the remnants of construction. Beverly beside him was in full bloom, no shadow of recrimination on her sunny face. He had made her happy. He revived in the certainty of it. The light changed and the clatter of traffic swelled like applause. Harvey Porter acknowledged the applause, but reminded himself that opening night is not the criterion. The test of real talent is the ability to sustain the quality of performance. He hoped that his feelings of guilt would not cross him up.

Harvey did not question his love for Sally though less and less often did he sprinkle this shrine with the holy waters of his passion. Drinking helped both of them lean into the mood for love, but sometimes they leaned too far. For a woman to go limp could be delightful. Different for a man. If forced to admit the truth, Harvey would have to say that he seldom stepped across the gray frieze runner that separated his bed from Sally's. And Sally, never. He could not remember when last she had come to his bed.

Properly. A shrine stays to receive the worshipper. Sally

was a superb woman, all spice and vinegar, no job too rigor-
ous, no sorrow too daunting. Her devotion had gently, like a
snowcap over geological ages, moved from the girls to him.
She telephoned his office if he was ten minutes late getting
home. On his meeting nights, she had a hot supper waiting,
herself waiting to share it with him. She read books that interested him in order to discuss them. A rare woman. Since
the heart scare he'd had two years ago (nothing; smoke in the
capillaries, the specialist had said; the cardiogram was fine next
day), he could see her in the window watching him as he
shoveled snow or fixed a tire. If she wasn't right out there
working alongside him. He was grateful for her care.

Sally had been brought up to repress her feelings, but
most of the acceptable ones had been acted out in the Porters'
second-story bedroom—a big, airy room with striped
wallpaper and old cherrywood furniture. As a bride, she was a
white sacrifice on a bloody altar. Later, resentment made her
stiff under her husband's beseeching hands, imploring mouth.
This had receded into a sympathy that encircled him sooth-
ingly, apologetically, sometimes, alas, deadeningly. The
triumph of her job, and capacity to support a failing husband,
activated her (it was also, Harvey thought, a pre-menopausal
surge of sexuality) and quirkily, maddeningly deflated him
until he recovered and they attained a short but memorable
balance that was close to the shared joy they had had at only
one other time in their marriage: when Sally had a hungry
womb to fill. Then she was a wholehearted partner in the act
of love. Once she had borne their daughters, she became a
dutiful wife and dutiful mother of enough children, though
determined to deny their father no particle of his proprietorial
rights to her. He admired the tact and grace with which she

submitted to him. Now that they were both past fifty, the
turmoil behind them and both still in health, Sally's sense of
duty included an accounting of tribulations shared. She owed
her Harve his pleasure, much as she did not dream of saying
No when Suzy called a year ago needing two hundred dollars
for an abortion. Harve didn't cross the rug very often but she
never said No when he did.

Harvey looked up, saw the Smithsonian Institution, felt
Beverly's hand, soft and warm, in his, and suddenly gasped
from a crush of guilt. But he blew it away. A man could be
unfaithful without being disloyal. Sally was safely ignorant and
he trusted himself to die before he would hurt her. Truly, he
thought, he had been dying a little before this amazing (he
looked again at Beverly, alive and clear as a mountain spring)
coming together. Can it be, he thought with elation, that I am
a crepuscular animal?

Harvey didn't mind the Impressionists as light refresh-
ment between solid meals of Rembrandt and Velásquez. They
agreed on four rooms of Impressionists and not a glance
elsewhere. It was an exciting decision: Impressionists first,
lovemaking later. They hurried up the marble steps.

The pleasure for Beverly was to be there with a man who
was not doing her a favor. She was not his burden. He was
with her by choice. She knew these choices were never accidental. But they were in a museum and not in bed, so she
knew that what she had for him was more than her willingness
to lovemake.

"I guess what you like about me is my élan, huh?"

"Yes," he said. "Your inimitable élan. Are you sorry that it
isn't your high IQ?"

"Don't worry about how I feel. I'm not so sensitive."

"But I do worry. How you feel is of primary importance to you and therefore to me because you mean so much to me. Do you know how much you mean to me? I want to know you will fight for your feelings."

She promised she would.

They walked around the pool in the rotunda, cooled by the mirrored marble shining gray as calm eyes all around them. They stared with awe into the perfect proportions of the dome that spread like a blessing over their heads, and agreed—for once—that they were in a beautiful place. Harvey led the way to Gallery Eighty-five, where there were four paintings by the one Impressionist who satisfied him, Degas the intellectual.

They stood in front of the Duke and Duchess of Morbilli.

"More than the chair back separates those two," Beverly said. "She looks so gentle and sad. He looks like a passive aggressive snob."

"You should bear in mind that the painter was her brother. Maybe one of the Duke's relations would have seen things differently."

"I know what I see in you," Beverly announced as they moved to a Manet. "It's that you know everything."

"I'm not afraid to share what I know. You may have noticed that."

"Yes. But I don't object to pedagogy."

His pleasure came across so plainly that it almost embarrassed her. They stood before Manet's *Old Musician*, and Harvey said the children were Polish refugees. "I don't know if they were Jewish Poles," he said, "but I do believe that the picture is based on a pop art theme of the time—Courbet did one, too, I think—that of the Wandering Jew."

"I'd like it anyway. And I know you're going to like those Corot landscapes, right?"

She left him for Monet and Renoir. The Impressionists were vibrant enough to shatter glass. She had to blink. Blinking, she was well pleased with herself. She had always been able to curl around the edges of people and make herself liked (except by certain natural antagonists: anti-Semites, woman-haters, militant youth), and in truth she was skilled at making up to people. The point that was at this moment raising her toward a kind of sonic barrier of happiness was that in her Harvey Porter context, she was undeniably and unflinchingly herself. The Real She. It was a discovery. She would not have supposed that the Real She chose to bum around museums with a chubby old pedant.

Harvey finished paying his solitary respects to the flowers and fruit of Fantin-Latour and came to Beverly in Gallery Eighty-nine. The joy in his face as he came through the archway was more intense than the intensity of Van Gogh's yellows. She could not look at him, she was so ashamed, so unworthy of bringing that intensity of joy to the face of a man. She turned away, ashamed to look at happiness so naked. She would, if she could, have stepped into a frame and joined a landscape, for the responsibility of kindling such joy in the face of a vulnerable and trusting Puritan was beyond her emotional range. She hid among the high grasses in the depths of a Monet garden where light shimmered in a mild wind, and when she came out again she was able to look, almost straight into the joyous and loving face of Harvey Porter, and to accept his feeling for her and to absorb some of it. Delight leaped out of all the frames and danced in a circle around Harvey, who smiled, showing the little space between his teeth, and said, "I missed you."

Abandoned with abandon, Harvey stood alone in a more somber space and considered the provocative fact that every painting in that room—the most compressed to the most expansive—was enclosed in a heavy and ornate frame. There was a point to be made. He carried himself, on his small neat feet, lightly to a corner of this little butler's pantry of a gallery, where hung a wicked portrait of Paul Gauguin that had been painted by wicked Gauguin himself. It provoked the mind of Harvey Porter. Paul Gauguin had taken into his own nervous hands the frame of his life and broken it. He had jumped the track of a Sunday-painting wage slave and hurled himself into the wilds of consecrated art to slap those flat, insolent sheets of color in front of the horrified eyes of the gently bred, then died an ugly, possibly appropriate jungle death, perhaps too soon. Gauguin had not lived to be as old as Harvey Porter was now, but he had lived. Yet here he was, in a frame. Here were the head and shoulders, framed, of what Harvey might accurately describe as a shifty-looking character, detached and complicated. Maybe he felt guilty for having left his wife and children. But he had painted a halo over his head. Gauguin was in Eden with two apples dangling beside his sad eyes and his extravagantly twisted nose. He had made himself fantastic— divine, profane—and in his long, wicked hand was entwined a viny green plant that grew, as it curled through his fingers, into a serpent.

What could be made of that? Porter, the failed hero, asked himself. Did Gauguin know that Picasso would stand on his shoulders? Did it matter to him, recognition?

Harvey was over fifty-five years old. He had lost more battles than he had won. He would not break any frames. He would wait for his future. He would wait in Waddingford during the seasons to meet what came and he trusted he would meet it with equanimity.

"What do you think about recognition, Beverly?" She had just turned the corner and stood by him. "Delayed recognition, unforthcoming until one is old or dead?"

"Old is okay. Dead is no good."

Harvey was not dead yet. He did a strange, un-Harveylike thing. Slipped his hands under her coat and held his palms against her breasts.

She did not call the guard.

Beverly had found one of her favorites. She knew it from art books, a famous painting and, like her, just visiting in Washington. It was different in person. The watered blue of the little eyes. The pale flush on the cheeks. The washday colors were so unexpectedly delicate on this strong woman who had looked only stolid in uncolored reproductions. Now, looking down from the wall with her gentleness (*not* gentility) and unconscious dignity, she was beautiful. Beverly, color-struck, thought: *He must have loved her, after all!*

She was Hortense Fiquet, Madame Cézanne, painted by her husband. The story was that by the time he married her, he no longer cared for her. If it weren't for the child, he would not have married her at all. Cézanne's father disapproved of this fast, older woman from Paris and so they were not married until shortly after the old man died. By then, it was said,

Cézanne had stopped loving her.

Impossible. Beverly observed the freshness of her flat cheeks, the round arms, the quiet of her deep breast. He had feeling for her. He leaned on her calm strength. The plain face had thought behind it. It was a face that had the courage to live its life. Love me, love me not, Madame Cézanne was the kind of woman Beverly wanted to be. She knew she did not come close. Spunky and two-fisted, as she liked to think of herself, the truth was—as it spoke to her from the painting— that Beverly Peck Gordon had never taken a chance in her life. Even the seemingly daring novelty of saying Yes to Harvey had been a safe bet. A fair exchange left no debts to be haggled over. She had made it clear that she did not want to see him again. She would not suffer the discomfort of waiting for him. Furthermore, her supersensitively self-protective palps had divined for her the man in the world least likely to make the faintest ruffle on the lily pond of her life. Beverly did not make mistakes (though God forbid Sadie should ever find out about Harvey Porter!). She could step in a puddle, thumb her nose at a senator, lose her purse in a poker game, go to bed with a stranger, and always grab the next plane and fly home (which was exactly what she was planning to do that night). Under the grit of Madame Cézanne, Beverly knew herself for a coward. The last poopout of the courage of generations of wanderers and refugees committed to a harsh survival. The dying whimper of the diaspora.

Madame Cézanne did not feel the least bit sorry for her. Her expression was unsurprised as she looked down on Beverly.

"You are afraid," she said, in a very awkward French accent, "of the hooks of love." There was a certain high-

hattedness in her stance, a certain self-righteousness, too, that
Cézanne had caught. "You said so yourself," Madame
Cézanne reminded her.

He got down there between her legs and held them apart
and rammed his mouth, teeth, tongue up her tender cavities,
opened her wide and rubbed against her with his growth of
beard. It hurt.

"Peter. You're hurting me."

He couldn't talk. Up to his eyes in there. His tough jaw,
not recently shaved, grating her, his mouth pushing up into
her, the long animal tongue insistently licking as his back
humped over her and he came down heavily over her head,
upside down on her, wanting her to take him in her mouth,
urine smell, shit smell, and all, his thick, hairy cock to stuff
down her throat, she would surely choke on it.

This was lovemaking?

This was what she had to do to keep her husband interested?

This she owed him?

"Please. Please. Put your penis in me."

He flipped around. He slipped it in. He pumped. He
came.

"And you?" he asked. "Did you?"

"Of course," she said. "Oh, yes."

He flung himself over on his back, grabbed a ready towel,
wiped, and handed the towel to Beverly. Very soon he was
snoring.

But she remembered once, when he had found it hard to
come and he had said to her, "You're bigger than a subway."
Ever since then, though he was never impotent for long, she

had felt not quite right, not tight enough down there, and she tried to squeeze herself together to be tight on him when he came in.

Beverly envied Madame Cézanne the presence of a husband who saw so much in her. On the one hand, Cézanne was surely no picnic to live with. But on the other hand, Hortense Fiquet had managed to keep her cool—and his interest. It was right up there on the wall for everyone to see. Those Frenchwomen, Beverly thought regretfully. They knew how to see to the needs of their husbands. And the husbands were grateful. Cézanne had been grateful for the wifely ministrations of Hortense Fiquet. That was why he saw such beauty in her. Peter was not so grateful to Beverly and therefore he no longer found her beautiful. He had made that clear.

But less than an hour ago, Harvey Porter had turned to her on Eighth Street. His face was perfectly still and serious. "You are very beautiful," he had said to her. And she knew that he was right. Now she knew that he was just around the corner with Gauguin.

As they left the National Gallery, they did not look back. Harvey Porter did not envy Gauguin and Beverly would not for all the world and time have wished to change places with Madame Cézanne.

They were old lovers this time. Harvey need not have worried. Beverly's room at the Watergate Hotel was round, rounded with soft curtains, rounded off so that there were no corners for reticence or constraint. It was a ring of no contention.

A man past fifty-five and no satyr. But, in honesty, he was

not at all tired; there was no question of challenge. He had been stirred to an awakening of feelings that had been dormant for a long time and that he had not expected to rise again. It was, in his mind, a miracle. And with all this unlooked-for, shattering, ineffable crush of joy and desire, he felt also gratitude. When he made love to Beverly on the round bed in this ample room whose deftly neutral decor left the occupants free to create their own spirit, love it would be that was not a taking. This time there was something he had to give her.

"My love is a red, red robe," she said from far away in a centered armchair that swiveled. She sat swiveling, utterly pleased with herself, in her white underthings—white bra, white bikini pants, sparkling as a detergent commercial, no doubt rinsed and quick-dried overnight in the clean American way. Sitting there, in her underwear, ripe and saucy, she looked to him like a piece of pastry.

"Not a French tart, I hope?"

"It is a matter of some amazement to me that a woman can be so wholesome and so sensual at the same time."

"How about because sex—or sensuality, as you would have it—is wholesome?"

Harvey, sitting on the perimeter of the daisy-spread bed, felt the rising of his heart with the growth of his sex. "I would give you an A for that response," he said, growing.

"Not scarlet, I hope."

He wanted to give her something she could keep. A standard she could carry, this suburban Joan of Arc. There were a number of things Harvey knew about her that she did not know herself. He saw the desperation behind her hopeful eyes and he knew that she was fighting for her life. He wanted, of

course, to save her. He carried his drink the wide distance to
the center of the room and set it on the round table between
the two armchairs. Beverly swiveled out of her chair and into
his lap. "I won't be too heavy?"

She was a Playmate now, full of affection, undoing her
bra to take his head to her breasts, kissing his soft hair as he
kissed her. "I want you to have all pleasure of me," she said. It
had been a long time since she had given that kind of pleasure.

He would save her with an infusion of his love.

She was Joan of Arc in white underwear. Listening to her
voices and uncertain about attending them, unsure of whose
voices they were and if they were up to any good. "Listen,"
Beverly of Arc would say, "a person could get into trouble
following strange voices."

Harvey would give her strength and courage. He would
teach her to value herself.

"You're going to upgrade me," Beverly would laugh at
him. "Make me an Alpha instead of a Beta so I'll look better
and live longer and get narrow feet and be accepted in the best
circles."

He wanted her to be happy.

Businessmen shave in the morning; lovers shave at night.
When had Harvey shaved, Beverly blissfully wondered. His
face was smooth against her skin, her breasts, and his kisses
were soft as love itself. When he stood up and took her into his
arms, she did not fall away from him. She did not brace herself
in her accustomed defense against being crushed. She had
settled into his gentleness. Enamored. Unarmored. She received and returned his embrace in a perfect stillness of trust.
She who had always been edgily uncomfortable in the pres-

ence of delicacy suddenly lost her peasant's stake in rough-
ness.

She was shocked at the swell of emotion that surged from
her and enveloped the man she was lying with, under, over,
across, curled around, enfolded by. He was dear to her: she
wanted to give him her life. "Oh my God!" she said on her
breath. "I love you. What am I going to do now?" All her
starch was gone. Her laughter and her derision. Beverly was
quiet. No longer in an adventure, she had struck reality. She
was naked, figuratively speaking, for the first time since her
birth. Harvey was not so surprised as she was.

"You don't ever become a different person," he told her
insistently. "Everything you are now or will be was there to
begin with. Unexercised."

"I never felt like this."

"You have become more of the person you really are. It
has happened to me, too. We have reached great heights together. And great depths of ourselves. You have given me
life."

Beverly wept against his chest.

Why was she crying? Was this not her dream? A nifty kind
of love, Harvey Porter's love, in that it made no demands on
her. Love that did not ask her to love him first or best or
forever. Love that did not expect her to take care of him or
listen to his troubles, fan his vanity, fulfill his social obliga-
tions, or see to his physical comforts. Harvey already had a
wife. So this was free love, no freight to pay. A real experience.
Why was Beverly crying? She had a husband who would be
waiting for her when Harvey went home to his wife. She had
her wonderful life to return to. Well, in any case a good life—it
would be a crime to complain.

CHAPTER 10 _____

"I've been to London four times." They were lying together on
the round bed in the round room of the Watergate Hotel.

"Why do you tell me that?"

"I want you to know about my life."

"Oh," said Harvey Porter, a little abstracted. "How was
it?"

"London?

"London was nice. My life was nice, too."

She was moved by the way he seemed to be trying to look
around and under and over her eyes. Trying to find something
he knew was there and wanted to get hold of. Minimizer, she

thought he was nearsighted and too vain to put on his glasses. That was Beverly. Always making molehills out of mountains. That he could see her straight and love her was hard for her to believe.

"My life is still nice," she said. "Now that I've finally had a lover, it will be better.

"How many extramarital lovers have you had?"

He was very quiet. "Four," he said quietly. "No. Five."

"Counting me."

He nodded.

She wrapped herself in the top sheet. "I'll catch up," she said. "I'm younger."

Wise guy Beverly. She made him wince. *Brava*.

"It seems to me that your children must benefit enormously from having a mother so alive and outgoing as you."

"I don't know. My son wears only cashmere sweaters. My daughter goes to catered parties at her friends' houses. They go to a school where there are no black students, let alone teachers. They think every kid in the world has his own stereo set. In short, Harvey, I don't think I've done so well by them."

Harvey was up now, tying his robe. She was wearing a sad twist of sheet. Twisting sadly in it, she took his hand to her lips.

"The hardest time in my life," Harvey said, looking away, "and the most exciting, was when I changed careers. I was deeply involved in my studies. Sally was taken up with the challenge of earning money. My girls had to learn to take responsibility for themselves . . ."

"Yes. But that's not the Jewish way. If you don't run everybody's life, you're not a good Momma."

"Did you love your parents, Beverly?"

She rubbed his arm against her face. "Did I? I do. I'm not as old as you are, remember. My parents are still alive. Not so much older than you." She rolled close to him. He stroked her hair.

She had very little voice in her. "Will knowing me," she whispered, "have compensated for some, for any, of the disappointments in your life?"

He thought of his daughters. They wrote to their mother. *Love to Dad. My best to Dad.* Two cards on Father's Day. Two Christmas ties. He thought about justice—Warren Hamisch and Lieutenant Giordano. Suzy then and Suzy now, still unable to find firm footing: he was still afraid for her. Suzy. And Bruce Czajkoski. NMI.

"I don't believe, as you do, in patterns. But I think that our experience has been more real than ordinary reality. I think that having known you will nourish me for the rest of my life."

She wiped her eyes on his shoulder. "I can't believe I'll never see you again."

He got up and went to the window, a long, curtained arc overlooking Virginia Avenue with its traffic islands like a peaceful flotilla.

"That I will come across a picture someday or a piece of writing that I want you to see, and I won't be able to give it to you.

"Or something nice will happen to me that I'll want to tell you about. Or something terrible, and I'll need you . . ."

He did not turn around. She talked to his back, broad and motionless in red velours.

"And someday I'll read on the obituary page that you have died and I will go on living in a world without you and that

you've never really been in for me. What do you think is
sadder, Harvey? A world without you? Or with you in it and we
never see each other?"

He did not turn.

Beverly apologized. She was a sloppy crier. Maybe that's
why she had given up crying at an early age. "Listen," she said.
"Oh, God. I'm sorry to be carrying on like this. This is not
what I expected.

"Easy come, easy go," she said. "Excuse the pun." Years
of tears were falling.

"Let's forget it," she said. "If we'd had another month, we
could have had a fight and I would learn that you were boring
and you would learn that I was bitter and we wouldn't have
liked each other so much any more and it wouldn't have been
so terrible to say goodby. We would have been glad to split. In
a month. Or two months. Three at the most."

Harvey went to the dresser to look at his watch. It was
five-thirty. Her plane was to depart at seven-fifty, his at eight-
ten. Beverly watched his face in the mirror. When he turned it
to her, he was composed.

"I was not unhappy before I met you," Harvey said, composed. "I had learned to live with quiet satisfactions."

How long would it take Beverly to decide that Harvey
Porter was too slow, a bit tedious with his long talks about his
daughters, too wrapped up in his family, no self-starter?

So much of the present cued him in to the past. He talked
about his ancestors, the Early Americans. His own childhood
and his dead parents were close to the surface of his mind.
When would Beverly start to be dissatisfied?

For who would want to spend the rest of her life listening
to music with a man who loved Berlioz and walking beside a

man who loved tall trees and knew all their names and the names of the birds who sang in them? How would an active and curious woman like Beverly adjust to the body rhythms of a man used to standing still in open fields and sitting quietly by a fire, breathing low, with no nerves to keep her stepping?

Harvey Porter's life had been lived in open spaces. On broad, level planes, under the breath of clean sky. He knew the names of flowers and butterflies. The crunch of autumn leaves was in his footsteps as well as the cruel softness of deep snow. Harvey had lived out of doors as much as inside. He had sat for four or five hours on grass in hot sun—not fishing, not reading, but unfenced in his contemplation of limitless horizons and unlimited dreams. For most of his life Harvey had been in places where he could take long walks without ever having to turn a corner. He had seen woods full of trees that no dog had ever peed on. He could sit on a rock beside a stream without a policeman's stopping to look him over or the encroachment of an insinuating stranger, looking for company. This open life, Beverly had apprehended early on, makes a difference. A person gets a chance to think things through. A person is calm with himself in space and time. He can look back to where he has been and maybe see ahead to where he is going, He may arrive at some understanding of who he is and what he wants from the world . . .

Beverly had grown up in narrower places, with close walls, low ceilings, and doors that led only into other small and overfurnished rooms. Her expanses stretched to no horizon further than the roofs of the buildings across the Grand Concourse or the smoky end of the line of traffic toward the Third Avenue Bridge. Grass grew in narrow rectangles between the chalk-marked sidewalk and the dog-shitted curbstone and it grew short and sparse, littered with cigarette stubs and candy wrappers. It was impossible to get to a place where there was nothing but weather and room to sit in it. Even Orchard Beach took a sweaty trip and another trip back on crowded buses and subways and when she got there it was full of other people wanting pieces of space to crowd into pieces of time. Proportioned to these narrow ways, Beverly was therefore uneasy with expanses. Vacancy was a threat and solitude an enemy.

She had traveled more than Harvey. To London four times. To Greece. Israel. And she had seen America first. But she had always brought with her the tight dimensions of her parents' apartment and her husband's house. She had always traveled under auspices. Only in the past two years, since she had wandered in the subterranean expanse where the walls had receded when she reached to them for support or direction, had she begun to suspect that life could be wider. For the walls had pressed in on her, but when she reached to them for security, they fell away. What good were such walls? That's what she learned from her Bar Mitzvah depression: that no matter how close you built your walls, they were not there when you needed them. In the past two years there had been time—Peter busy at the office, his social life strung increasingly on a business key, the children taken up, going off, and her own depressive torpor having prevented her from filling the holes as other housewives filled spaces on their shelves and lines on their social calendars. And in this unaccustomed time and space she had come upon a few relevant, unexpected, and curiously reassuring facts about herself. For example, she liked Art. Beyond what people were talking about. Bumbling through museums and galleries, she discovered that she was passionate about the shapes of things and the juxtapositions of colors; the mood, the viewpoint, the choice of objects. Beverly, given open time and space, learned that she liked art and did not like social circles. She liked school and did not like shopping. She liked doing things rather than watching them. She learned to see life in people's eyes and did not like to be with dead-eyed people. She liked her house and family but did not like to be the spinning center.

But moving out was hard. It was hard to escape the compression of deep carpets, thick draperies, hanging fixtures, jutting ornaments. They squeezed her in. Sadie Peck squeezed her in. Sadie had confessed only recently that she had never let Child Beverly out of her sight, had followed her down the Bronx streets, into the park, into the playground, to the school gates. "You were such a beautiful child," Sadie said. "I was always afraid you'd be kidnapped." Peter Gordon, of course, squeezed her in, seeking to quiet his own fears by protecting the life out of his wife, thumbscrewing Beverly with his anger at every outward move she made. All the Nicely-Nicelies squeezed her in, like Mrs. Griggs, the housemother at college, who had cautioned her against appearing barefoot in the dormitory living room: "We don't want our boyfriends to know *everything* about us before we're married."

But the strongest opposition came from Beverly herself.

From her upbringing as a genteel Jew, she had habitually rebelled in a very genteel manner. She had become comfortable in a thumbscrew and had grown to its shape while screaming and wriggling to get out.

"The thing about a gilded cage," Peter Gordon had remarked at a recent dinner party, "is that somebody keeps putting in the birdseed." Beverly had agreed with her husband.

Moving out was hard. Unlike Harvey Porter, Beverly had never wandered through a day of nothing but wind and fields. She had a lot to learn from him. The pity was that he could not stay to teach her.

There was a cropped carriage she liked, a horse-drawn black chaise heavy in the foreground of a Degas painting in the Boston Fine Arts Museum.

Harvey knew it. He said it was a family portrait and he liked it, too. He went so far as to compare the picture to certain stories by Henry James in which the narrator stands, like the carriage, strongly in the foreground of the story. Beverly promised to read the stories as soon as she could get them out of the library. She could see what he was saying. She could hardly wait to read them.

Then she remembered that she would not talk with Harvey again.

"Couldn't we find some way at least to write?" she begged after they had dressed without using the dressing room beside the bathroom. "Couldn't I send you clippings or anonymous notes? To your office?"

When his face closed he didn't look angry. He looked like a statue of a patriot.

She hated herself for hurting him.

He said he could not take the risk. Sally was a jealous wife. He could not take the risk of hurting her.

"Of course, of course." Beverly apologized. "It would be crazy. Please don't feel bad." She did not let herself cry.

She had no rights to claim. Furthermore, she had no real wish to keep a connection that could only complicate her marriage. She did not know why she was carrying on. Where did all her new faces come from? What happened to the heroine of two nights ago, the brilliant proponent of the one-night stand—or, to be more accurate, the one-night lay? Where was that Beverly who wished at all cost to avoid the hooks of love? She had got what she wanted. Why wasn't she out front, taking her bows?

Harvey Porter was right, of course, prudent and wise. What possible long-term connection could be made by people so far apart, geographically and ethnically, as they? How fortunate, in fact, was Beverly to have found a one-night lay with the integrity of Harvey Porter! These things were not accidental, she knew in her cells. She had mystically and deliberately chosen a man who would not spoil things for her. Who was this new Beverly whose heart was out in a storm and who thought she could make room for Harvey? It didn't have to be a lovers' communion. She only wanted to know him. She would have to work hard to keep remembering how tenderly he had treated her. This new Beverly was a crybaby.

It was time to call for a cab. She watched him pick up the dapper telephone with the dial in the handle. He was a gray-haired, lined, potbellied man who would soon be old. She loved him past all her efforts to laugh herself out of it. She listened with pleasure as he called for the bellhop: the fine voice with an effortless dignity that promised matched luggage in the best leather instead of her stray overnighter, which she could easily have carried out herself. She said nothing when he put down the phone. He watched her say nothing. Ambering light filtered the wide arc of curtains. The soundproofing was very effective. Harvey and Beverly stood apart, soundless.

She could make room for him.

When things were bad, there was a diagonal crease in his forehead. "I will never forget you," he said.

No other man had ever shown himself to her uncostumed and unconquering. She did not want to lose him.

"Your generosity. Your incredible honesty. I am alive as I have not been for many years."

She would never see him again.

He came from behind and held her against him. "People can't live on the heights," he said. "We have to live on flat land and to settle for ordinary satisfactions. Which are beautiful satisfactions." He meant children. Friends. Books. Gardens. "You have a husband who loves you and needs you," he said. "You have two beautiful children."

He was right, of course. Most people settle. The happy people settle. She felt his love and his deep sadness. "This is torture," he said. He took short breaths like a man with a chest wound.

Beverly pulled away from him. "I won't settle!" she cried.

Harvey knew what he was doing when he worried about goodbys almost before they'd had a chance to say hello. Harvey was an expert at renunciation. Beverly saw that. Harvey was in love with pain.

Beverly, thinking for herself at last, thought she must be in love with life. She had been playing hard to get, but it was time for her to make a declaration. She would not settle.

"Such a big mouth," Sadie used to nudge her. "Let somebody else do the talking. You'll stay out of trouble that way." Beverly was ready to defy Sadie and speak up. Forty-year-old women-of-affairs don't have to do what their mother tells them to. Beverly would speak out. You got a big mouth, use it.

There were one or two things she might like to talk about. Art was okay on the side. But there were a few things right down the middle, very close to home, that she had been overlooking. Before she could move toward art, or in any outgoing direction, she'd have to get that center space cleaned up. She would have to open her mouth and put things in order. Peter Gordon, for example. She would have to open her mouth to him.

> "Sir, you and I must part,—but that's not it;
> Sir, you and I have lov'd—but there's not it;
> That you know well: something it is I would,—
> O, my oblivion is a very Antony,
> And I am all forgotten."

Man, we has got ourselves all mixed up in a mess of interdependency, I don't know how we gonna get out of it. You gotta let me out from under that ol' thumbscrew.

It's your move, my dear. The thumbscrew is not pinned down.

You mean I could of went whenever I wanted?

Yowzah! Thumbscrew ain't clamped down.

And all I'd have to do is walk away?

Mais oui. La porte est ouverte.

Yeah? And what would you do then, Billy Boy, Billy Boy?

What would you do then, Charming Billy?

I wake to sleep and take my waking slow.

I learn by going where I have to go . . .

Oy vay! That blows my mind!

Ah, love, let us be true
To one another!

She would have to open her mouth to the whole family.

The Gordon House Commune
General Rules

1. No dope on premises.
2. No division of labor by sex or age.
3. Confrontations at Sunday-night house meetings only.
4. Weekly menus and shopping lists to be turned in before 9 A.M. Mondays.
5. Dinner guests signed in one day in advance.
6. Kitchen cleaner responsible for garbage.
7. General cleaner responsible for vacuum bags.
8. Absent jobholder responsible for replacement.
9. Individuals responsible for own bedrooms.
10. Special dieters responsible for own meals.

Now that Beverly was no longer playing putty and filling in all the cracks in her household, she stood suddenly alone in the middle of her life. She had lost all her excuses. "Put up or shut up," said her walls and windows. "You're on the spot," said the kitchen stove. Suddenly BPG was responsible for the conduct of her life, accountable to nobody but BPG herself. It's all yours, baby—love it or leave it.

She looked over her shoulder and no one was there.

So she had to open her mouth to Heightsville:

Ladies and Gentiles:

I'm so proud to be standing here on the speaker's platform

with all the bigwigs on this memorable occasion of the commencement of our wonderful ninth-grade children from their wonderful Heightsville Junior High School.

It's so nice of you all to ask me to come.

First I want to thank our wonderful president of the ninth grade, Brayne Stallion, here, for his very flattering introduction of Yours Truly as Class Mother of the Year. Thank you kindly, Brayne.

Next we heard Dr. Darlington Crack, our extinguished principal, announce the results of this year's standardized achievement tests, which showed our Heightsville youngsters to be considerably ahead of ninth-graders from the Chicago slums, the poverty pockets of Appalachia, two Indian reservation schools, and certain southwestern schools dealing in dark-skinned Americans of Mexican descent.

Then we heard Willington Screw, our meretricious superintendent of education, who concluded his short peroration by warning us parents to keep a close eye on our teenagers, all the more imperatively because the City of New York is only twenty miles down the road, rising there to threaten us all with its theaters and concert halls, artists and intellectuals, its foreign neighborhoods and strange foods and unconventional praying places, and its dirt and smoke and noise and danger and life.

These illustrious professionals have expressed every sentiment of importance to us parents and students of the Heightsville Junior High commencement class. All I can humbly add is a word for the future, a charge to the class of our fine, young, clear-eyed, openhearted young people as they stand in their white dresses and dark suits poised on the brink of Senior High School.

Boys and girls, you are privileged to be commencing here from Heightsville Junior High. We are all privileged to be living in Heightsville. All of us must fight to keep our privileges. You, your parents, and all the citizens of our beautiful town deserve the very best. We deserve it because we can pay for it. The Jews have already pushed their way into our town. The Gentiles who couldn't stand it have already moved farther up the river. The brave ones who are left have gallantly joined hands with their Hebrew brethren and both kinds of people, Jew and Gentile alike, are working together to keep the niggers out.

We have built our High School on solid rock at the far end of Heightsville, where it was most expensive and least convenient. But we built that school for a higher purpose. We built it to keep far, far away from the problems of communities less fortunate than ours, like Burntwood with its embarrassing questions about integration, equality of opportunity, democracy, and sharing the cake.

Nevertheless you, the younger generation, no less than we, your parents, must remember your responsibility to move along with the times. We Heightsville folks, with so much to be thankful for, owe it to our community to keep in step on the march to the future. It would be remiss of us, your parents, merely to tell you young people to go on to Senior High and make good grades so you can get into top colleges and keep hold of your privilege. We tell you that, sure. But we also remind you to think about the larger world, the longer future, and the greater good. All of us, great and small, rich and poor, dark-skinned and fair, crooked and straight, live in this one world and you youngsters had better keep that fact in mind.

Therefore, I charge you, Citizens of the Future, to get

together, get out and gather bricks. Gather bricks, I say, and pile them high. Build us a wall, Junior High School commencees. Build us all a big, high, and mighty wall around Heightsville! And keep the bastards out!

I thank you.

Beverly bowed with deepest irony. The applause was thunderous.

After she had straightened out those few things, Beverly would see about finding her place in the world.

She would be ready to think about that. She would return to Heightsville with gifts from Harvey Porter. Not a new woman, but a woman who had been newly introduced to herself. She would accept her new aspect with customary hospitality.

She did not need Harvey Porter. Nor Peter to turn into another kind of man. What Beverly needed was to draw herself out from behind the trimmed bushes out front and the pile of laundry in the basement, out from down her children's throats and from under Peter's thumb, in all of which places she had been trying to hide. Out even from her own threat to escape into another depression. Once out in the open, Beverly would have to bear the light on her. And in the glare of that light, she would have to take the decision to make a life for herself.

"I'll be able to do it because of you," she told Harvey Porter. They were at the National Airport again. Having crossed the strip of taxi platform under the flickering lights of landing planes and night coming on, they walked across the ground they'd met on. The same taxi, driven by its night driver, was pulled up beside the strip. Nobody noticed the youngish, carelessly dressed woman hurrying along beside the older, carefully put together man, walking close as they moved straight through the random cuts of fellow travelers going this way and that, seeking transportation to someplace or other. It was a chilly night but neither of them was aware of it.

They were at the airport again. They had gone from her place to his place and their bags were beside them. They had crossed the main building and passed the electronic sentry and walked to the end of an outstretching corridor, unaware of the cold cement, the brash signs and markings, the mothers and babies, people in wheelchairs, businessmen, students, honeymooners, tourists, adventurous matrons and guilty fathers and middle-aged lovers passing among them, unnoticed and unknown. Beverly's plane was boarding. They stood at the gate. "I am calm and strong," she told him.

Now it was Harvey who could not speak.

She touched the tips of her fingers to the tired place between his cheek and his eye. People hurrying by them were nothing but racing shadows. A current, a whiff, not there; periphery was suspended. "It is excruciating," Harvey said, and for a fast moment Beverly thought: "To be loved is all."

She thought, for just that moment, that she could not, after all, leave him. At that moment a claw stretched up out of the pit of her groin and ripped at her belly. So that she would know for the rest of her life, from that moment, what it would feel like to die.

To be loved is all? They could look out to the airfield where the jets streamed out and smothered her question. Beverly looked for the last time into the eyes of Harvey Porter, who loved her. She could see that he was dying, too, and she could give him no comfort.

She kissed him once lightly and once again. And he kissed her, taking her face for the last time in his very clean, soft, and most expressive hands. Man and woman held themselves together until the last, urgent boarding call, when Beverly picked up her bag and walked out on the airfield. She thought she heard him calling her, but she did not look back.